READER BEWARE!

<u>THE ADVENTURES OF HEMERA NYX IN THE GALAXY OF THE FUTURE!</u> IS AN ADVENTURE NOVEL SET TEN THOUSAND YEARS IN THE FUTURE AND DEEP IN OUTER SPACE.

THIS NOVEL IS FOR ADULT READERS ONLY. IT CONTAINS GRAPHIC DESCRIPTIONS OF VIOLENCE, DRUG USE, ABUSE, ASSAULT, MENTAL HEALTH CRISES, AND OTHER MATURE SUBJECTS.

READ AT YOUR OWN RISK.

=[RSK]=

"BY ALL THE GODS, *GO!*"

The final command of Lenna, Estro of Fortress Nyx, barreled across the docking platform like a cannon blast, cutting to silence as the thick glass doors slammed shut. Sturdy metal teeth began separating on the other side of the vehicle airlock, the hissing of outer space rising to a howl as it consumed the escaping air.

The emergency void-raft's hatch refused to close as a large man struggled with a young woman who roared a single word with an outstretched hand, the sound dampening into a single point of horrified ardor.

"MOM!"

Beyond the glass airlock the muted scene erupted into chaos. Doors and hatchways slammed open, ripped from their frames as bloodthirsty passengers flooded the wide hangar floor, silently frothing inarticulate screams, their limbs grasping for revenge.

Lenna turned her back to the horde and placed both hands on the glass, the X-shaped scar across her face twisted with worry.

Her daughter's outstretched hand closed in a tight thumbs-up as she fought against the man, a painful, mirthful smile on her face, sobbing as she shouted silently back.

Her mother's scar lines smoothed as pride filled her eyes. The hint of a smile danced at the edges of her mouth, then twisted in pain as the first of the hands grabbed her.

And then there was a snap.

Every light on the *Imperion Konkero* flared, blinked, and strobed a thousand-billion points of lights and colors. The overloaded bulbs exploded into showers of glass shards as the photonic detonation stabbed its way past the young woman's eyes, the gruesome brilliance frying the insides of her skull.

The man's strong arms overtook her as the hatch slammed shut, the void shrieking to silence as it pulled the small spaceship deep into its soft embrace.

Crashed on a hostile alien planet, a lone human girl fights for her life! Will she rise to her destiny, or will this fiery hellscape be her *doom?!*

Hemera Nyx

In...

The Trial by Starfire!

```
==============
[TIME: 12047:07:14:14:06]
==============
[LOCATION: UNKNOWN]
==============
```

[STATUS: DYING]

```
==============
```

====== [START] ======

Twenty thousand light years from Earth, an ancient ball of flame rages in the cold, empty void.

The wrathful star was a roaring droplet of light and heat from some long-forgotten cosmic explosion, embittered at its isolation, stewing in indignation at its deep exile. But this angry ember wasn't completely alone: chained by gravity, a tiny mote of dust spun around it, unable to escape.

That dust mote was a planet twice the size of the Earth. Its rotation and orbit, both far too close and far too quick, scorched and fried the massive rock in its cosmic dance of death.

And yet, *life*. The most mysterious of galactic miracles laughs in the face of impossibility. The surface of this extreme planet was a patchwork of superheated nightmares saturated with plants and animals, all consumed in the universal business of biology: eating, reproducing, and being eaten.

Rocky mountains made of translucent jewels glowed incandescent in the oppressive light. Between them, forests grew deep into steep valleys, filled with scaly ribbon-trees that chirped as they slowly shuffled about, digesting nutrients from silicate microbes. Black rivers rushed and gurgled, spilling out into an ocean made of bubbling oils that reflected shimmering rainbow-like clouds high in the transparent sky. Under the oils swam unthinkable things, creatures without need for breath or light.

In some places, deadly deserts shifted, the sand made of crystalline fragments that disintegrated anything caught in their endlessly refracted light; in others, fungi-like jungles dripped with slime, hungry parasites hiding in nests within nests, waiting for their next meal to walk by.

And on one charred, rocky outcropping overlooking a deep, spongy valley, something familiar: the remains of a human spaceship. The void-raft lay smashed, smoke streaming long thin lines that plateaued high in the atmosphere as it roasted under the wrathful star above.

A human figure shuddered amongst the wreckage. The harsh coral light bore down on the white-and-orange pattern of an emergency spacesuit, an overlay of metal joints and skin-tight synthetic fabrics: a child's sized suit stretched on a teenager's body. Alarms beeped and pinged inside the metal and glass helmet as she struggled to regain consciousness. Her closed eyes jerked erratically, ragged breathing echoing in the small space between her face and the glass as the temperature continued to rise.

The young woman was dying.

======[CONDITIONS: EXTREME]======

Consciousness returned to the young woman slowly, the electric storm in her skull receding to an aching background vibration. Her fingers flexed instinctively, feeling stiff material around them. Something over her head echoed her labored breathing back to her. Her heart thrashed wildly.

A sharp pain shot through her as she tried to move her left arm. Groaning, she instinctively tried to rub away the static that burned behind her eyelids, but her hand landed on something flat and smooth instead. Pulling a sticky eyelid open, her blurry vision could just make out the outline of a glove resting on a clear barrier in front of her face.

Beyond and high above, dark shapes floated in the deep, flaming sky, blocking some of the intense light. Something about the fluffy shapes triggered a memory, a single word recalled with a stab of synaptic pain.

"Cloud." She forced the word out, her tongue thick and dry, the sound trapped. Something fast ripped overhead, blocking the sky for a fraction of a second. A trail of smoke and fire followed as a hard thud shook the dusty ground.

She could feel it now, all over her body: the metal skeleton and tight synthetic fabric, bulky boots, pads at her elbows and knees, the weight of a helmet pulling her head back. There was some sort of hard box on her back, keeping her torso elevated, while a small chest-plate pressed down hard, compressing her lungs.

The clouds rolled across the sky, revealing the full force of the flaming orb. She winced and rolled her head, searching the gray, dusty ground around her, but twisted smoking steel and shattered glass boxed her view in.

Her head was too heavy to lift, so she shifted uncomfortably on the hard box attached to her back, huffing the stale air inside her helmet. And then she was wide awake, her addled brain filling with a singular crisis.

Air!

Her eyes shifted in and out of focus as she scanned the up-side-down view of smashed and overturned crates and shredded hull, only to start at the sight: a handled flat box stuck out of the charred ground.

Something deep down inside knew she needed it.

She needed it *now*.

Pushing as hard as she could, she swung her arm over her body and rolled onto her side, grunting in sobs as the useless air rushed in and out of her lungs. Her head swirled, the edges going black again as arcs of pain rippled and burned through her leaden body.

Inhaling deeply through her nose, she began to crawl. Dark shapes streaked overhead as the ground shook again, but the young woman was too focused to notice. Gasping now, her skin and muscles burning, she dragged herself forward with her good arm, her heavy boots wriggling in the dusty soil.

It was getting hard to see as she arrived at the small box. Arm shaking, she reached out and felt the connection, a slight buzzing tug as her gloved fingers wrapped around the handle. A muffled beep sounded from outside of the bucket on her head as a small display on her glove's forearm lit up. Her vision faded in and out, her dry mouth wide and panting as she tried to read the bright words:

```
=======
[POWER LANGUAGE ORGANIC TRANSPONDER]
=======
[NAME: HEMERA NYX]
[CIN: G-FN-RA-12-9799-5]
[STATUS: ALIVE]
=======
```

A tiny pinprick of hope stitched in her chest at the same moment a metallic *ping* startled her. Inside her helmet, just above the top end of her visor, a display strip began scrolling words in a faint alarm-red.

```
=======
[!WARNING!]
=======
[!SUIT POWER DRAINED!]
[!MEDICAL EMERGENCY!]
[!EXTREME CONDITIONS!]
=======
```

The warning alerts continued to scroll by, each with a loud metallic *ping!* Recognition flared in her gray matter; sparks flew behind her eyes as she peered at the object in her hand, forcing the sounds through her dry, thick lips: "Pee. Ell. Oh. Tee."

It was flat and boxy, about two fingers thick and at least two hands wide. One side had a small electronic screen displaying information, something she couldn't see as her vision wavered and darkened. The thick handle sparkled in the same square-triangle pattern as the palms of her gloves.

Deep, rasping breaths clawed at the useless air in her helmet as her eyes lost their focus. Without thinking, she rolled to her side and shoved the **PLOT** into a slot in her chest plate.

Nothing happened.

She pushed again, then slapped the handle and twisted, her muscles threatening to quit, her lungs flaring. The handle followed and locked the **PLOT** into the socket with a satisfying *click*, followed by another *beep.* Coolness began spreading over her body as the whooshing sound of air and fluids stirred gently near her skin. Fresh air flowed into her helmet as light blue words flashed above her visor.

```
            ======
      [OPEN:  NON] [SOAP:  NON]
            ======
      [GRAV:  3.2] [PLOT:  006]
      [TEMP:  325] [LIFE:  001]
      [ATMO:  7.9] [ESRA:  000]
            ======
      [12047:07:14:14:09]
            ======
```

Her exhausted eyelids closed as she took a long, gasping breath and passed out.

======[SCENARIO: CATASTROPHE]======

Hemera Nyx woke up. Every cell in her body was in pain as she lay in the dirt, a coolness flowing over her body in waves. A slight breeze of fresh air tickled her face, calming her outraged senses. Gray dust pressed against her visor, the darkness a relief from the oppressive flames above.

As her eyes fluttered in the renewed oxygen, Hemera could hear the box on her back working hard: small clicks, whirring, hissing air and gurgling water being pushed through small tubes and permeable fabrics, the mechanized exchange of inputs and outputs, hot and cold, taken and expelled. The vague idea came back to her with a sharp stabbing in her head.

Life support.

Clicking filled her helmet as new words appeared in a tiny display along the edge of her visor, slightly obscured behind her deeply sunset-yellow hair as it pushed in around the edges.

One display read:

```
======
[SUIT OVERLAY ACTUATED PROTECTION]
[AUTO-DEPLOY: ACTIVE]
======
```

Another *click*, and her attention was pulled back to a different side-display.

```
======
[OPEN: NON] [SOAP: YES]
======
[GRAV: 3.2] [PLOT: 005]
[TEMP: 328] [LIFE: 032]
[ATMO: 7.8] [ESRA: 046]
======
[12047:07:14:14:13]
======
```

"UuuuUUGHHHaaaaa..." The sound escaped her lips involuntarily as her emergency spacesuit constricted. With a sudden impulse, the metal supports that ran up and down the suit sprung to life, shoving Hemera away from the ground and straight upright.

"...aaaaAAHHH!" Hemera cried out as her shoulder popped into place. The world turned fuzzy and spun as it exploded into a shower of sparks. An incredible pain shot through her injured shoulder as a wave of nausea flooded her guts. Gripping her shoulder tightly, Hemera's eyes adjusted as her visor darkened, dampening the intense light as she gasped at the view.

"Oh my gods..."

The star dominated the sky, a god's eye peering down upon her with unbearable heat and pressure, an ocean of flames in space encircled by a vibrantly black horizon. Her knees buckled in awe, unable to stand before the presence.

Raising her good arm to try to block the light, she tore her hurt eyes away and looked out. Translucent stone mountains lined the long valley thick with tall, pillar-like trees that floated blue ribbons into the oppressive atmosphere. Tree-dotted hills moved slowly in the distance, a low rumbling and high-pitched squeaking between them. One hill was crawling up the side of a mountain. More clouds roiled off on the horizon, growing ominously darker. And something... something else was flying around in the sky, wiggling through the atmosphere, the sudden shadow overhead vanishing among the thickening clouds.

Hemera's slack jaw mumbled of its own accord.

"...where the gods-hell am I?"

======= [HELP/HELP/HELP] =======

Chunks of twisted metal, glowing hot around the edges. Padded seats tossed about like discarded toys, some broken in half, their synthetic fabric charred and smoking. Boxes and containers scattered, their contents spilled and shriveled in the intense heat. All evidence of familiar human constructs was melting and burning in front of her.

Hemera closed her eyes to keep the existential panic from overtaking her, but her attention was drawn to the the small speakers jammed against her ears, the tinny cacophony of a living alien world invading the privacy of her mind. The soft thud of her backside hitting the dirt hardly registered in her awareness. She was overcome with the whooshing of air around her, sharp clicking noises from the nearby trees, dangerous cawing above her, and something else... a whining, barking sound. Something in pain. A wild alien cry for... *rescue?*

Hemera slammed her hands on the sides of her helmet, but the sound persisted and demanded her attention. For all the feral exigency that threatened to end her fragile emotional state right there in the dirt, the painful yipping pushed past her defenses, calling to her, driving her forward. Keeping her eyes downcast, she scanned the wreckage once more, trying to locate the sound, unconsciously grateful for the sudden purpose in her life.

"I'm here... I'm coming... where are you?" She breathed the words to herself, the sound bouncing back hot and dry from the thick glass in front of her face. Her glove gripped the edge of a dented cargo box, but as she tried to pull herself up, the box flipped, sending a long, thin pipe flying into the air. It stuck upright as it landed in the gray dusty soil, shiny brightly in the intense light.

Hemera's eyes lit up as she leaned over to scoop it up, the gravity nearly pulling her off balance. There was a beep as her gloves made contact with the metal studs that dotted the tube. The sounds of crying faded as her fascination with the device saturated her awareness. It was nearly as long as her forearm, with an indented spine along one side. One end of the cylinder was an intense series of small lenses with an elevated ring of small magnets. On the other end of the tube was a simple hooked ball. The tube itself had a large red button with two knobs on one side, with only a small switch on the other.

"I know what this is..." she breathed to herself as she examined the cylinder, tilting to read her forearm display.

======
[RADIATION ASSISTED MAGNETIC ARRAY]
[P:782] [D:12]
======

The big red button was too tempting.

Click.

Hemera yipped as a brilliant beam blasted out of the lenses, carving a fiery line in the dusty soil as she stumbled backward. The line followed her fall, carving an almost-molten line along a chunk of steel wall.

Releasing her grip as she nearly fell, Hemera's heart was throbbing. Her head spun again, her breathing ragged and dry as the world threatened to go dark. She recovered enough to look at the device again, whispering to herself.

"It's a RAMA... it's... it's a beam-cutter. And... and a..." Her gaze followed the tube down to the other side, her thumb reaching the small switch faster than the part of her brain that made good decisions.

Click.

"OOF!" The tube extended at a shocking speed as the hard, hooked ball slammed into her gut, the force of which caused the **RAMA** to pop out of her hand and land in a puff of dust two meters away.

"Oowww..." Hemera rubbed her stomach tenderly as she shuffled towards the device. A pry bar nearly as long as she was tall lay on the gritty ground. She reached for it as she bent forward, but the pull of gravity was too much and she stumbled to the ground.

Shuffling around, Hemera got her knees under her as she grabbed the device. Clicking the switch to retract the extension, the knowledge came flooding back: this was a standard maintenance tool for... to maintain... *something.*

Mental hands grasped for more information in the darkness of her mind when a sudden movement caught her eye - something struggling under some melting wreckage, wriggling and crying, the source of the cries of pain. Hemera hastily crammed the **RAMA** into a half-open leg pouch as she shuffled forward, getting her heavy boots back under her, unconsciously gripping her injured shoulder.

"I'm sorry... I'm sorry. I'm here. I'm here. Just let me..." Wrapping gloved fingers around the hot, jagged edges of what appeared to be some sort of cockpit console, Hemera began lifting with her good arm, only to stop and step back, smacking her visor.

"Use the tools!" The rod shot out again, but this time towards the edge of the wreckage. She could feel the struts of her suit stiffen and push, helping her lift as warning beeps echoed in her ears. The creature struggled and dug at the ground as she gave a final shove. The wreckage toppled backwards, nearly taking her with it as she fell to

her knees right in front of the being.

Millimeters from her face, separated only by glass, was an alien.

"Oh, wow..." Hemera whispered as she slowly leaned back. "You're *beautiful.*"

It was half her size, a four-legged animal covered in shimmering white feathers that rhythmically rose and fell. Its head was long and covered in prismatic scales, the flashes of blues and greens a welcome relief from the red and gray landscape.

Two small white eyes held her for a moment, then the beast lowered its head. Hemera hesitated, then reached out. Her gloved fingers gently stroked the creature's scaly head, but all she could feel was the inside of her glove. It bowed again, then turned away. Limping, its spiked tail dragging, she saw a back leg bent in a different direction from the rest. A large gash ran the length, oozing thick blue blood that hissed in the atmosphere, the vapor rising gently upwards in a thin steam. Hemera felt the delayed impulse to help, try to treat the creature's injury somehow, but the grateful creature had already limped some distance away. Worse, even in the blankness of her fried and scattered mind, she knew she did not know first-aid for aliens.

The desperate reality of Hemera's situation began seeping into the corners of her awareness. She retracted the extended pry bar and placed it back in her leg pouch. The creature limped past the remaining wreckage and started across the dusty clearing towards the woods as Hemera felt her body shaking as the terror gnawed at the edges of her mind.

"*Where am I?*" she breathed to herself, smacking her sticky mouth together to summon moisture, but it only made her throat hurt more. Exhausted, Hemera looked around the wreckage once again, trying to remember where she was, or how she had gotten there - anything to push away the panic that threatened to drown her.

Something had messed with her brain. All of her memories had been pulled beyond reach, an electric wall between her and who she was. And without memory... there *it* was. The weakness in her knees. The trembling. Death by Fear was coming for her, and there was no one to save her.

"Where is everyone?"

The sky darkened quickly for a moment, the artificial whine of engines and thrusters filling her ears as she leaned her head-bucket upwards, her eyes growing wide. A small spaceship was hovering over the crash site, leaning gently to one side, a metallic helmet scanning the wreckage from the inside of a small cockpit.

"...aaaaaAAh! AH! AAHH! HEY! ME! PLEASE! HERE!" Hemera stood as fast as she could on weak legs, straining to lift her waving arm high.

The pilot nearly missed her, but to her relief, she saw him do a double-take. The wounded alien tried to scramble as the spaceship landed on the far end of the clearing, which puffed with dust as the boosters fired and landing gear thudded. Hemera stumbled forward as fast as she could, only to fall to one knee as she caught her breath, her life support squeaking and gurgling as it tried to keep up.

Panting hard as she knelt in the dirt, she raised her hand to block the light. The stranger's cockpit was already open as they reached and twisted, pulling a **PLOT** out of the console and inserting it into their chest plate. A blast from the bottom of their boots kept them upright as they clambered out of the cockpit and landed softly on the ground, casting a cautious glance around, trying to stay upright in the high gravity. Hemera raised a hand as the figure trudged towards her.

"Yes... I'm... here... please... help..."

The armored spacesuit seemed like it was from a distant age of swords and spears, the thick hammered plates of metal threatening in appearance. A piece of red fabric on the chest-plate flared in the heat, a stream of smoke rising as the human started closing the distance, face hidden in the darkness behind the helmet's glass, itself protected behind a grill of decorated iron bars.

The wounded space alien yowled and hissed at the newly arrived stranger, who jumped back in alarm and whipped a metal pipe from their back as they stumbled to a knee. The tube's thicker back end pressed into their shoulder as the feathered alien hissed again. Hemera panicked, a pang in her skull returning a memory to her as the hollow end of the pipe started to glow. She roared in alarm.

"NO! PLEASE! IT'S NOT A THR-"

The horrifying sound of concentrated energy shredding atmosphere and flesh filled the thick air as the beam ripped through the creature. The alien gave a gurgled cry as it thrashed, then fell still under the rising haze of blue blood. Hemera couldn't move as she panted, tears mixing with sweat, eyes stinging against the matted hair that stuck to her face.

The human watched the dead alien a moment longer. Seemingly satisfied, they turned back towards her and advanced, swinging the rifle around so the barrel pointed at Hemera's chest. Her grief began giving way to confusion, and then a cold, paralyzing dread. The human raised their hand to their steely helmet and flipped a switch. Copying the movement, Hemera reached up and found a small switch on the side of her helmet. A rough voice cut through the sudden static that filled her ears.

"-ound one."

Hemera took a breath. The human gently wrapped their hand around the grip, finger on the trigger.

The barrel began to glow.

Her lips tried to articulate her confusion, but her mind was paralyzed with the last icy thought of an animal not knowing why it was going to die.

A deafening screech vibrated the inside of her helmet, causing her to scream in fright, the two screams reverberating together in her skull. Something large swooped in from overhead, landing with a thud next to the alien corpse.

It was a monster from a child's nightmare. Leathery wings spread wide, its body covered in spikes and black feathers. It had a bright purple beaked mouth with huge white eyes that reflected red in the light. It wasted no time as it dug large, sharp claws into the white-feathered carcass, thick horn-beaked mouth slobbering as it consumed flesh, feathers, and blood with voracity. The human stumbled backward in terror as a finger squeezed the trigger. The shot meant for Hemera missed by less than a meter. A cloud of dust and rock covered her as she watched the scene unfold, unable to move.

The alien stopped eating and turned at the sound of the blast, then rose up to its full height, evaluating the space-suited human as they stumbled backwards, trying to bring the hot barrel around.

They were too slow. The alien rushed forward, knocking the gun aside as long talons slashed into the spacesuit, cutting the metal plates like cardboard. Their screams echoed in Hemera's helmet radio as the alien shoved its beak into their guts, the sound of fabric, metal, and flesh ripping as it tore the human in half. The spray of blood and organs covered the ground as the alien began greedily slurping them up. Hemera breathed to herself at the gristly scene.

"...holy shit."

The alien jerked its head away from its meal, a blood-filled helmet firmly in bony jaws as its large eyes searched. She gasped as she tried to switch the radio off, but it was too late - it saw her, still on one knee, covered in dirt. The human's helmet crushed like a tin can between powerful jaws. The monster spat it out as it scrambled towards her, winged claws matching the pace of hind legs, a predator's sprint towards doomed prey.

Hemera grunted as she struggled to her feet, only to stumble back to the ground. Crying out at the pain in her shoulder, she grappled with her suit and the ground, flipping and scooting backwards until her life support smacked into a piece of wreckage. The alien was upon her now, rising up high as wings extended. Black pinpoints in large white eyes held her in a hungry gaze when a glint of metal caught the corner of her eye.

Hemera reacted on instinct, hand snatching the device and pointing as the alien screamed and rushed forward for the killing blow. Gloved fingers fought for the button and pressed as hard as physically possible. A brilliant beam shot forward towards the creature, only to stop short, the cutting energy held back by some unknown force. The creature stopped, backpedaling slightly at the unexpected light and sound, unsure of what to make of this new thing as it snarled in rage and hunger.

Hemera hyperventilated as she fumbled with her other hand, a searing pain shocking her body from moving her injured shoulder. Gloved fingers, thick and trembling, grabbed the knobs and twisted. The beam retracted, quickly becoming a glowing nub only a centimeter high. The monster emitted a clacking sound as it moved forward for the kill. Hemera breathed in as hard as she could and twisted the knob in the other direction. The beam shot forward, slamming into the creature's leathery skin and shiny feathers. It screamed and stumbled backwards, lighting up in a spray of colorful flames, quickly becoming engulfed in smoke and fire.

Hemera held the beam on the alien monster, screaming her incoherent rage as if it was the one responsible for her suffering, everything she'd lost - all of it. The flaming creature struggled as the beam bore down and burst through. The alien fell backwards, spasmed in the dusty soil as liquid sprayed over the charred ground as it twitched, flopped, gave a muted cry, and fell still.

Gasping for breath, Hemera gave herself to her panic as she staggered to her feet and scrambled blindly into the truly alien forest.

====== [SEEK SAFETY] ======

She ran until the world swirled around her; the dizziness drowning out the last screams of the evil creature still echoing through her head.

The tall ribbon-trees shaded the forest floor, a relief like twilight from the overwhelming light of the fire-god in the sky, but the shifting shadows made it difficult to see. Hemera slammed into a scaly trunk and bounced off, then wheeled around and sprinted blindly farther into the woods.

Up ahead, small cliffs and caves made of large gem-like rocks jutted out of the ground, half-visible in the darkened scene. She instinctively made towards them as one of her large boots caught the edge of a root, slamming her head-first into the soft ground. Still panicking, she crawled forward until she made it under the rocks as far back as she could go.

A few moments in the dark of the rocky shelter settled her panic. She curled up into a ball as the relief gave way to crying. A few more moments passed as her body unclenched, muscles shaking, her breathing calmer.

Soothed by the hiss and bubble of her life support, her eyelids soon became too heavy to fight.

```
======[SIGNS OF LIFE]======
```

The small light from Hemera's helmet display filled her eyes as she opened them again, very much against her wishes.

```
           ======
[OPEN:  NON] [SOAP:  YES]
           ======
[GRAV:  3.2] [PLOT:  005]
[TEMP:  326] [LIFE:  032]
[ATMO:  7.8] [ESRA:  046]
           ======
   [12047:07:14:14:42]
           ======
```

The semi-translucent rocks she shivered and sobbed under, the gray and dusty ground, the chirping of the ribbon-trees. The weight and bulk of her suit, the gurgling of her life support, the uncomfortable awkwardness of her helmet resting on the ground, and the hard chest-plate that constrained her. One small thought rose inside her, the center of gravity anchoring her current reality.

"This is a nightmare."

Hemera remained curled up, unwilling to move, unable to think, incapable of remembering. Existence seemed a curse, the universe heavy and hot, hostile and deadly.

Gradually, she heard new sounds pressing in against her ears. A wobbling, croaking sound. Buzzing and fluttering. A thin whooping kind of snap. Something deep and rumbling.

Peeking an eye open from behind the thick glass of her visor, Hemera saw the forest alive with all varieties of life. Even from beneath her rocky shelter she could see creatures no bigger than her thumb climbing the scaly trunks, snapping at even smaller insects that fluttered and sped by.

Above, the thicker clouds dragged dark shapes along the ground. As they passed by silently above, the shadows erupted in life. Strange plants blossomed in moments, opening wide petals and cups, expelling motes of light.

Spider-like lizards ambled along the ground, ripping up and eating the plants that retracted too slowly behind the cloud. Winged things landed in the bright blue ribbons of the scale-trees, ruffling them up, tearing a few in toothy beaks only to take off again.

Even the atmosphere, caught between vapor and liquid, seemed alive somehow. Thick bands of languorous heat were layered with bioluminescent motes that floated along curling currents in the dark shade of the forest. A whisper of awe escaped her lips as she reached out, swirling the thick air and sparkling dust with a gloved finger.

The enormous red ocean of fire above the trees had shifted, and the mottled lights on the forest floor traced lines in the dusty dirt. The sky was so clear that she could see the spotted darkness of space growing along the far horizon between the trunks and ribbons.

There was that low rumble again. She quickly forgot about it as she began trying to unclench her body, stretching out her sore and knotted muscles, massaging her shoulder gently, trying to coax it back to life.

Another gust. That whooshing, uncomfortable sound: uncontrolled atmosphere, like a maintenance tunnel, but… *more*. Hemera felt the push of a breeze under her rock as the trees swayed, their ribbons twirling around each other. Closing her eyes, she whispered to herself, trying to take stock of her situation.

"OK. I'm alone. I've lost my memory. I'm being hunted by monsters and maniacs... ...and I'm hopelessly lost on a roasting alien planet."

She snorted as she wrinkled her nose. A tiny chuckle bubbled up inside. Then another. Soon she was shaking in quiet laughter.

Help wasn't coming.

The human in the space-armor tried to kill her.

Help was trying to *kill* her.

She tapped thoughtfully on the toes of her boots. Stiff fabric fingers poked at the squarish metal tubes tucked up against the sides of the soles. She wondered what the small springs and gears were for as she did her best to not notice the abject terror of certain, approaching death.

Another rumble waved through the thick air. It felt slightly more powerful than before.

Shifting and wiggling, Hemera moved closer to the edge of the rocks. Pushing herself upright, she wrapped her arms around her knees and tried to scoot forward to get a better view of the moving forest. Each small creature caught her attention in turn, the bizarre forms of living things new to her, yet somehow familiar. She wondered if life itself contained something fundamentally the same across the entire galaxy.

A harder breeze blew in. The trees leaned slightly, then leaned the other way as if actively rebuking the wind. The hard wall that repressed her memories cracked slightly as the word came to her, one eye twitching at the stab in her brain as the word to describe the terrifying whooshing of air, the rumbling, the sun and sky came back to her.

Weather.

It was a memory. It was *something*.

It wasn't enough.

She let gravity pull her gloved hands down, which thudded hard on the soft ground. She tenderheartedly watched them, then twitched her fingers in their thick fabric, then caught her breath in renewed terror.

Her leg-pouch was empty.

She patted every part of her that could hold something. *Empty.* The fluttering in her chest picked up as she scanned the dark forest floor.

There. The glint of metal, alien and artificial in all the biology, barely visible as one end poked up from behind a tree root. Hemera was tempted to leave the thing where it was and shivered at the idea of leaving the relative safety of her rocks. But when she closed her eyes the image of the alien monster came back: rearing up high, wings spread, evil eyes boring into hers as it reached out with deadly claws.

Stretching her hand open wide at the distant tube, she wished she could simply *will* it into her hand. At that moment, as her fingers fully extended, there was that feeling of electricity buzzing into her glove, followed by a small *click*. The metal rod shook, then flipped over the root and flew right towards her. She yipped in alarm, throwing her arms over her head, and the rod dropped into the dirt three meters in front of her.

There was a slight pinging sound in her helmet as she peeked at the nearby tool, but she ignored it as she held a hand up high. Marveling at her new magic powers, she reluctantly came around to the idea that specific magic was most likely electromagnetism.

Giving another serious scan of the living forest, Hemera couldn't see anything that seemed like a threat. She shuffled forward, grimacing as cramps shot up and down her legs, her shoulder still stiff and painful. Grunting, she stood up into a run, quickly covering the distance to the rod as she reached her hand out wide. There was a *click* as the rod jumped off the ground and slapped hard in her glove, the fingers snapping around it in a strong mechanical grip.

"Whoa..." Her head swam for a moment as she backpedaled from the impact. Something had changed inside her helmet, an even more and louder pinging that stabbed at her skull. It only took her a second to see the new words scrolling by.

`======`

[!WARNING!]

`======`

[!LOW POWER!]
[!SEEK SAFETY!]

`======`

Hemera's mouth twisted at the command. Still, she figured conserving power was... was...

Her eyes lost focus for a moment as a stronger gust of wind swirled through the shaded forest. The trees groaned as they bent, their ribbons going wild. Shivering despite the heat, she turned her spinning eyes back to the rocks, back to safety, only to freeze in terror at a dark shadow in the exact spot she had just been.

It was *her*.

Sections of her own white and orange emergency suit, ripped and shredded, flapped in the gathering wind. The helmet latches had rotted off as the shattered glass visor swung on squeaky hinges. Her own bleached skull grinned a wide smile back at her, its curly rings of yellow mummified hair matted, flesh dissolved in the poisonous atmosphere. A naked, bony hand offered a warm welcome as it lay outstretched, a promise of true safety under the rocks.

Hemera shook her head so hard the world swirled around her, then looked again. There was nothing under the rocks but deep, soft shade. She looked back out into the alien forest. The trees had moved, but it didn't matter - lost was lost. She took a step away from the rocks, then another, a simple thought rattling around in her head.

"I'm not dying here."

====== **[ANYWHERE ELSE]** ======

Blindly walking forward was the only option, so deeper into the alien forest Hemera trudged, the soft dust cushioning her heavy footfalls. The screeches and calls of alien insects and birds piped into her helmet, matching the volume of her heavy breathing, which was occasionally overtaken by the *rumbling* that was now deeper and more punctuated.

Somewhere in the back of her mind, Hemera could see the small spacecraft her attacker had left behind, still parked near the wreckage... covered in the gory spray of human remains, the burned body of an alien monster sprawled nearby.

The *person*. Hemera's boots plodded dully on as her scrambled brain replayed the image of the space-knight. The massive sun continued its march towards the horizon as she tried to hold it together, replaying the memory of the spaceship landing, pulling the **PLOT** from the console...

Her eyes picked up and scanned the seemingly endless scaled trees that slowly shuffled about. The rising lightness of panic spread through her limbs like an icy fire, unmooring her not just from her immediate surroundings, but from reality itself. In this forest, on this planet, in this galaxy, in existence itself: Hemera Nyx was completely and absolutely lost.

But still her mind churned, replaying the memory again. The

knight extracted their PLOT. They put it in their spacesuit. *Then they... there was... a burst that had kept them upright as they jumped from their ship...*

A strong rumbling vibrated her skin as her eyes traveled down her legs, but it took another minute of looking before her brain latched on to what she was seeing: four independently swiveled squarish tubes connected to the sides of her boots. Hesitantly, she leaned over and poked a tube with a gloved finger, fighting the dizziness from the intense gravity that pulled down on her without mercy.

Nothing happened.

Hemera huffed, following the lines of the struts up her leg to what seemed to be a button on each knee brace, and her gentle extended finger returned to a fist as she slammed both buttons hard. The tubes on her boot sprung and wiggled to life, and Hemera felt a gentle push upwards. The small but powerful engines seemed to wait for command.

She took an enormous breath, looking around at the endless shuffling of scaly trunks, the relentless chirping of creatures and plants. It was impossible to keep any direction except one: up.

It happened in an instant.

Unsure of how to engage the small boosters, she leaned back, only to be met with a blast from below. She yelped as the back of her helmet slammed into the ground, then gasped in surprise as her feet launched upwards, dragging her upside down into the air. The world swam and faded as the blood rushed to her head, causing her vision to dim into redness.

The thrusters cut off. Her helmet hit the ground like a ripe coconut, her body following after like a pile of wet clothes.

"Uuuughhh..." she breathed, half-open eyes staring up at the blue ribbons that rippled like water above. The blast had startled the local wildlife into silence, with only the rush of another hard breeze filling her ears. Even the trees themselves seemed to shuffle away, giving her a better view of the dark starry sky above, the ocean of flames turning dark pink, inching ever-closer to the horizon.

Vibrations from her boots continued to jiggle her legs, rousing her from her stupor. And there was that growing rumbling, the sound of muffled explosions rolling across the landscape, howling after her like a new deadly monster that she could not see.

Every inch of her was exhausted. Her muscles burned, the tendons and ligaments stretched and injured. Even her brain seemed ready to abandon her, neurons firing erratically as it struggled to keep up with her surroundings. The vision of her own dead body under the rocks filled her mind as she fought the temptation to go to sleep... to just... give... up...

An adventurer stands up when all others lie down.

Hemera frowned as the words surfaced from somewhere deep inside of her. The line wasn't hers. A pang hit her gray matter as she suddenly saw herself holding a book. The paper pages had yellowed with age, lines highlighted, the margins filled with scribbles.

"What's slowing you down, kid?" Hemera breathed softly to herself.

And then it occurred to her that she wasn't dead. Not yet, anyway. She was, in fact, still alive. That meant there were still options. A smile twitched on her face, seized by a sudden curiosity to find her limit. Hemera versus the world. How far could she get? Was there really any other choice?

One of her boots lifted off the ground as if it weighed nothing, the tubes gently thrusting at the ground. A soft roaring began working its way out of her as she started wiggling, rocking back and forth, engaging her exhausted muscles that had quit moments prior. The rumbling had continued to grow in volume, the time between larger roars filling with the call and echo of smaller roars. She could feel it in the ground as well as the air now. An instinctive itching in her nerves urged her to get up, to get moving.

There was no time to do this delicately, no space for careful experimentation. With a shout, Hemera pushed her boots up again. The rockets flared to life as she shot upwards feet-first. The blue ribbons rushed past her as she flung herself farther up and up. Just as she felt like she was going to pass out again, she pulled her knees to her chest, flipped, then shoved her feet down as hard as she could.

======= [FLIGHT] =======

It worked.

"Haaa... hahah... *HAHAHAH!*" Laughing wildly, Hemera hovered a few meters above the waving blue ribbons, her shaking arms out-stretched in triumph and imbalance. The blood in her body surged and waned, but she held on, her boots wiggling, leg muscles tense and twitchy. The swiveling thrusters compensated for her movements, and soon gave her a sense of stability despite the intense gravity in-sisting she return to the ground.

The world outside of her protective suit glowed with alien intensi-ty as the overwhelming sun, now an offensively bright purple, contin-ued to slide down the horizon. The clear sky behind it thick with stars, blending in with the glowing motes from the forest drifting upwards in the growing twilight. They twinkled and danced in the air, their wobbling like the inside of a blast furnace expelling its heat. A deep, persistent rumbling gave the impression that the entire planet was broiling in a royal, feral fire.

She slowly spun away from the purple sunset. The rocket boots hissed and clicked as her twitching lessened and her legs stabilized. She continued to rotate slowly, overawed by the alien landscape. She had never felt so alive, so clear, so in-control of her life as her entire reality crystallized to a single point: *survive.*

But as she completed her turn away from the sun, her exaltation evaporated. The weather - the *storm* - had grown so large it formed an almost solid mass that towered so high it touched space itself. The thick, rope-like strands of raging wind and fluid whipped and rippled as the thunders piled up on each other into a single, unrelenting vi-bration. It was a churning tidal wave of destruction, and it was headed right for her.

She might have lost herself in the sight of it if not for a line of smoke, pressed on by the growing winds, suddenly engulfing her. Her eyes followed the line down, and down, and down. There, nestled among large stones and small shrubs, something familiar: the remains of a large human spaceship lay smashed and charred, the chunks of hot steel glowing in the shadows.

Shapes moved in the darkening purple light. Searching. Flashlights. Checking corners. The blast of an energy rifle. Nearby, a smoking pile of stiff spacesuits, helmets missing, flesh and bone...

In the nearly-vanished light, a glint of a glass cockpit hatch caught her eye. The void-crafts were the three-sectioned type, with sets of stubby wings and tail fins, like a fighter jet and a space shuttle had a tiny spaceship baby.

The cockpits were empty... and open.

======= [FIGHT] =======

Her body leaned forward, but the powerful pull of the planet caught her off guard. She panicked as she flipped, then flipped again, and finally caught herself, vision spinning as she shook her head. She was flying right at the crash site. Flying at men with rifles... but there was *no time*.

A massive bolt of lightning slammed the ground like an enraged giant's stomp. The searching men broke and ran for their ships, the storm now close enough to see from ground level. She was nearly there, yelling incoherently at the slamming hatches, roaring as boosters shoved spaceships into the air.

Another armored spaceman's ship rose as a thick bolt snapped a wing. The ship wobbled, then threw its engine under it. The atmosphere rippled as it shot upward, then snapped straight as it shot out into space, the lights blending with the stars, the color of exhaust and smoke lost in the storm that had the face of death, fluid with lightning and rage.

There was one left. The ornate armored suit glowed golden in the darkening purple light, a small stream of smoke rising from a patch on the chest-plate. Hemera aimed her head at the ship's open door. The ornate space-knight didn't see her - their helmet tilted upwards, away from the almost nuclear-level storm, tracking another single-seater that was speeding in their direction.

Hemera's eyes widened more as this new ship quickly whipped its primary engine under it with only a few meters left, resulting in an impressive display of thrust and fire as it quickly slowed, straightened, and landed solidly.

Unlike the stark hulls of the others, this one was handsome, decorated with some kind of custom paint job. It had dark brown and copper red streaks on its body and stubby little wings. Something about the way it looked, the white underside, the cockpit's brown-and-yellow pattern... It looked like *hope*.

There was a startlingly loud *PING!*

```
=======
[!POWER LOW!]
=======
```

One heavy boot dropped as it sputtered off, throwing Hemera into a spin as she fell to the ground. Sharp in her frenzy, Hemera staggered to her feet and ran forward, gasping for breath.

The man from the colorful ship scrambled out and landed hard on the soft ground. His spacesuit was almost cloth-like compared to the golden knight, who regarded the newcomer coldly. The new man regained his feet and stumbled angrily towards the knight, clicking the radio button on the side of his helmet. Something about this new man...

It all seemed to happen at once. The new man pulling a small gun from a holster. The sky filling with screeching leather-winged aliens. Her helmet lighting up with warnings. Her boots thudding in the heavy gravity. The roaring of thunder rattling her body.

Then she was on the golden knight, who jumped back in surprise. Hemera closed the distance as they swung a fist at her head. She dropped to a knee as the fist bounced off the metal bucket on her head, her hands already wrapping around a handle strapped to the knight's thigh. A decorative knife snapped free as she shoved forward and slammed down on his leg. She cried out in pain as her shoulder seized up and the knife deflected off an armored plate.

Then the knight was lifting her up. Squeezing hard against her rubber neck protector, he didn't move as Hemera punched and kicked. Her eyes locked on the grizzled features of an older man almost lost in the shadow of his caged helmet. A demonic and scarred face warped by rage and hate, watched her struggle behind the veil of reddish smoke rising from his chest.

Hemera fell hard on her back as the knight was snatched backwards and lifted high. Sharp claws and beaks tore and eviscerated the old space-knight, spraying her in chunks of spacesuit and viscera.

The haze thickened as the bombardment of lightning pounded the ground with the impatience and howling of a toddler's tantrum. Hemera tried to wipe the blood off her visor as she looked at the dead man's ship, only to see more aliens clawing at the metal, shredding it in the strobing light. Stumbling to her feet, she turned to see the cloth-suited man scrambling backwards in the dirt, firing his little pistol at the alien rising up high before him, wings outstretched, plasma bolts punching small smoking craters in the monster's skin.

Small flowers of electricity bloomed on the edges of her suit as the swell of electric moisture grew static crystals. She started sprinting, wild past pain and exhaustion, pushed by desperation and adrenaline. The painted single-seat space vehicle sat just past the man and alien, the cockpit open and waiting, the warm light radiating for her.

It was the only spaceship left, and it was *right there*. The last of her strength shoved her forward. She was no longer worried about danger and far past the assessment of risks. There was only one clear path forward. The alien barked in surprise as the first of her heavy boots slammed into its back, then it flailed as she ran up its spiky ridge and jumped into the air, the sky behind her rippling with raw elemental rage. The last bit of rocket thrust flung her boot with superhuman power as it connected hard, the alien's head exploding in a spray of bone and blood.

"GET OUT OF MY WAY!"

Spinning as she stumbled to the ground, a blinding pain rippled up her shoulder. She could feel the heavy thud under her feet as the alien monster toppled forward, landing on the human who had been shooting at it. The man kicked and yelled as he tried to shove it off.

Hemera staggered, ran three steps, and then fell face-first into the dirt. Sucking in the roasting helmet-air, her wide eyes locked onto a single line that flashed a final warning as it faded away.

=======
[POWER DEPLETED]
=======

"No... no... no..." Hemera gasped. Grabbing hard at the ground, dragging herself with one arm towards the warm, open cockpit, grunting through the pain and exhaustion, she fought on.

Her helmet was dark. The high gravity was pulling her down. The inevitable, inescapable storm-wall of death was nearly upon her. It was impossible to hear anything beyond the reverberating roar of the dark, the flashing, the monsters digging into the dirt, the crackling flood of chemical rains ripping vegetation out of the ground as it rushed for her.

She couldn't move. It was too much. Far, far, far, far, far too much. Her muscles were unresponsive, her air depleted, her power gone.

There was nothing left to do but wait for obliteration.

======= **[THE END]** =======

And then she was up.

Something behind her had lifted her bodily off the ground and shoved her forward. Her sluggish boots kicked for purchase as they slid along the ground, her weary arms locking onto the edge of the cockpit for all their worth. The beating wet pump in her chest threatened to burst as she clung there, unable to pull herself up.

She rose regardless. Up, and then in. Falling hard between the saddle-seat and the hatch. Laying there. Stunned. The rushing thunder was muted as the hatch snapped closed. There was the loud clack of a latch locking shut. The small space instantly filled with rainbow bubbles that hissed on the blood and guts on her suit, chewing it into inert vapor and powder before vanishing. The intense gravity retreated as a chilly lightness rose in her body.

Hemera scrabbled up to look back out of the hatch window to see a pair of human eyes soft and joyful, the two almost-black irises familiar somehow as they hid behind graying curly hair, trapped inside a helmet that looked like hers. A peaceful smile spread across the man's face as he raised an approving thumbs-up, and then closed his eyes in acceptance.

The storm arrived.

======[THE SPACESHIP]======

Hemera slammed against the floor as the impact tossed the small ship high up into the air and spun it around like a toy in a tsunami. Her body was pummeled by the thick glass plates, then the floor, then the glass, then the seat, then the glass.

Time seemed to slow as the loose knife spun past her visor, the glyphic inscriptions glinting in the strobing lightning. Her fingers caught the edge of the forward monitor, giving her an anchor against the wild tumbles. The pain in her shoulder filled the edges of her vision with bright sparks.

Hemera grabbed the handle on her chest. Twisting and yanking, the **PLOT** device finally slid loose, nearly joining the rest of the loose bits flying around the cabin. She grunted and cried as her legs smashed into consoles and levers, and her gloved fingers threatened to slip loose.

The ship flipped again, and she used the shift in gravity to shove the cartridge down into the only slot on the console. The forward monitor beeped and flashed a warning as she slammed her faceplate up against the glass, trying to wrap her legs around anything she could find.

<pre>
           ======
    [ROYAL UNITED INDUSTRIES]
           ======
          [!WARNING!]
    [UNREGISTERED AERONAUT]
   [RESOLVE CONFLICT TO PROCEED]
           ======
</pre>

Her eyes shifted to the **PLOT**'s handle sticking out of the console as her hand slipped. Holding on with one hand, Hemera managed one final grunt as the ship flipped again. She half-pulled the **PLOT** out, then brought it down hard, screaming a wild howl of frustration and desperation as she twisted the handle to lock it in place.

There was a *ping*, followed by the dull clicking sounds of processors churning, barely audible over the roar of the storm. She watched the display scrolling as if in a dream, so far beyond exhaustion she no longer felt bound to reality as she held on with everything she had.

<pre>
           ======
     ...[...]...[...]...[...]...
           ======
    [AERONAUT STATUS OVERRIDE]
       [AUTOMATED DECREE]
     ...[...]...[...]...[...]...
   [IMPERION REGANTO: APPROVAL]
     ...[...]...[...]...[...]...
   [FORTRESS CONCLAVE: APPROVAL]
           ======
</pre>

[CONFLICT RESOLVED]
[FULL SHIP ACCESS: GRANTED]
======
[WELCOME AERONAUT]
[HEMERA NYX]
======
[!WARNING!]
======
[!HOME CONNECTION LOST!]
[!ISOLATION PROTOCOLS ENGAGED!]
[!CYCLING DISTRESS WHISTLE!]
[!RETURN HOME IMMEDIATELY!]
======
[LIFE SUPPORT: ACTIVE]
=============
[SYSTEMS STARTUP ENGAGED]
… […] … […] … […] …
======

There was a final *beep*.

======
[SYSTEMS READY]
======

Bright lights illuminated the thick rain and wind outside. An even brighter flare made the spaceship seem engulfed in light and fire as the four small thrusters wiggled and rotated out of the section hinges, blasting up and down seemingly at random. The center display switched to a digital horizon, which spun and flipped with the ship, the automated system pushing back against the chaos of the churning atmospheric detonation.

Hemera found herself suspended over the saddle seat, suddenly immune to the flipping of the ship. She body-slammed the padded seat with a hard thud as the metal struts around her legs snapped out and connected to mechanisms in the floor, followed by a final locking *click*.

The rear and largest section of the spacecraft ramped up a spinning, thrumming noise. Hemera felt like her brain was going to escape through the back of her skull as the primary engine erupted into a blast of thrust that sent her ripping through the clouds.

It was impossible to see anything outside the cockpit beyond the thick spray of liquids, the small cockpit strobing from the multi-colored lightning. Shackled to the seat, hands and feet pressed and pulled on pedal and handles, she watched the artificial horizon display jump and spin, unable to grasp what to do next.

Calmness and exhaustion seeped through her consciousness as she smoothly released her death-grip on the handles. The ship began to straighten itself. She let her eyes and brain do the work of matching the patterns between her controls and the ship's display, following her intuition, feeling it out. Soon the small thrusters pushed steadily downward, keeping the ship steady as it righted. The engine continuing shoving her higher and higher, the rush of the storm lessening with each moment. After a few more moments of adjusting, the front yellow nose pointed straight and clear, directly at outer space.

The first tendrils of intense crimson light peeked from the edge of the horizon as the tiny voidcraft sped out of the atmosphere in a puff of ice sparkling with tiny ionic-charged crystals.

The small scrap of steel and glass dashed aimlessly into the endless, star-speckled void.

======[OUTER SPACE]======

A calm peace washed over her as she swam naked in an ocean of stars, spinning and floating between the light and the dark, her flesh transparent, her body made of dust, ice, and fire.

The nebulae and gas clouds sparkled like mists of bejeweled dew. Small clumps of light and heat pulled together into bubbles that sparked, flared, and then popped, sending more effervescent dust and bubbles out into space. The far-away galaxies spun freely, luminescent pinwheels more numerous than grains of sand sprinkled in the dark infinite.

Her heart touched upon peace, but as she glided through the created universe, a heaviness grew inside. Anti-stars began pulling and anchoring her, limiting her freedom. Soon, the discontent spread through her spirit as a chill ran through her. There was something else there, among the stars.

It was the Void. The cold and the dark was with her, swirling and entangling. It shone deep nothing - no starlight, no swirls of incandescence.

Pure black.

Abject terror.

She screamed, the fires of creation burning in her throat. The cold continued to seep in, the stars inside of her dimming and dissolving into the blank nothing. Bending inward, Hemera pulled her remaining light together. Condensing heat, squeezing, constricting, until was all that was left was a single star. The void paused, just outside the touch of warmth that radiated from her.

It was enough. She could keep this small bubble of light up forever. She could be safe, here, holding onto this ember, the only remnant of what was once a vibrantly alive universe.

Standing still, holding on to the fire, she looked around once more. She saw the absence of all things, the endless nothing surrounding her, ready to swallow her whole. And then she felt a tug on her chest. Just behind the ribs, the fluttering of wings. Voices, laughing from somewhere within.

Music.

She opened her sternum and a bird burst out, giving her a fright. The flapping pile of feathers flew about the darkness for a moment, then came to rest on her shoulder, small talons ticking her, the gently chirping beak nestling against her cheek. She smiled as she petted the tiny bird, which cooed and warbled in return, each seemingly grateful for the company in their loneliness.

Her chest was still open, the light and sounds flowing out like a door to a party. Inside was everything missing: Faces, filled with love. Voices calling her name. A bright, glassy spaceship, alive with music. The safe place she used to hide in. A group of friends happy to see her. A blue and white orb, specked with greens and tans, saturated with warm fresh air and sunshine.

She roared as everything within rushed out, speeding outwards into the void. In an instant the dark was full of stars once more, ever more bright and sparkling, the fieriest campfires, the gods of the living.

The universe had returned, but it was all outside of her. She reached out her small, fragile hand at the distance. It would be difficult to travel so far into outer space alone. Life and death would be in the balance at every moment, every decision weighted.

Not quiet alone. The bird on her should chirped excitedly as it flew around her, fluttering and singing in a puff of feathers. Then it landed on the top of her head and let out a long, warbling note that she instantly recognized.

It was the call of adventure.

A reasonable person would have paused to consider the distances, the mysteries, the incredible dangers, but she sang along with her feathered friend, already moving forward. There was no time to waste.

Hemera Nyx was a Space Adventurer.

=======[THE VOID]=======

Consciousness came painfully.

Everything hurt. Every fiber of her body had been pushed far past exhaustion. Trying to move only highlighted the locked up muscles, the strained and swollen tendons refusing to budge. A gentle static filled the space, hissing a white noise. She tried her eyes instead, letting them focus on the small bright dots outside. Somewhere in her foggy brain the reality came to her.

I'm in outer space. Slowly shifting her head, she began trying to rotate her shoulders. Only one responded. Taking a deep breath of the cool air, she grunted, feeling the pain in her torn-up throat. She fought to regain control of her body but soon realized she was mechanically locked into her seat. Shaking weak hands ran up and down the length of the padded saddle-style chair, eventually finding a button.

Beep! Her spacesuit's external skeleton released its hold on the seat as the artificial gravity lifted. She floated upwards, the momentary sensation of falling causing her to cry out in pain as she wiggled. The panic quickly calmed, and soon Hemera felt more at peace, her strained body grateful for the relief.

Outside the cockpit, the massive crimson star had shrunk to nothing. It was hard for her to see the small, bright dot among trillions upon trillions of other dots. In those dots, too many to count, her eyes followed imaginary lines, filling in details, creating shapes. There, a face. And a starry thumbs-up.

And then she doubled over, grief hitting her heart so hard she wheezed in pain, the unexpected onrush of mourning washing over her confused mind. Choking on tears, she let her eyes wander the cockpit, looking for something familiar to ground her in her new reality. Every small console station, the messes of knobs, buttons, and levers, the small electronic displays that seemed almost randomly scattered throughout... it was familiar, somehow.

Hemera felt the sticky dried sweat on her face as she gently struggled out of her suit, caked as it was with the sterile dust of former blood and dirt. She let her gloves, boots, and life support pack float as she removed them, and soon the small space filled with suspended sections of her spacesuit.

Freed from restrictions, Hemera felt even more buoyant. The cockpit, aglow from an assortment of electronics that blinked, buzzed, and pulsated with various colored lights, gave her a sense of safety so clear and obvious that her new nakedness felt better than wearing the tight, chafing spacesuit. She stretched as best she could, looking out into the velvety starscape, vibrant in nearly every color she could see, more dots than she could count in several lifetimes.

It was all very, *very* far away.

She reached out and switched the gravity dial on the seat back on. Floating gloves fell to the floor with a thud as small bulbs embedded at the edges of the cockpit glowed softly, pressing her down with a chill that made her skin prickle. She breathed easier, even as the return of gravity hurt her muscles and organs from the previous overexposure.

Then she noticed the source of static - a little station on her left with a microphone, speaker, some various knobs and dials. A small monitor displayed wobbly lines in red, blue, and green on a tan background. There was one large button at the base of the displays, right next to a microphone that jutted out of the console. Hemera pressed down the button, and the static stopped.

"Saluton," she said, her voice cracking and weak from strain. "Saluton?"

The gently hiss of static replied. She tried again.

"Saluton, this is Hemera Nyx. Is anyone there?"

She released the button again, and the static returned. A deeply buried memory rose in her. *Static is the noise of the universe being born.* The universe was a *shhhhh* - soft, smooth, and unresponsive.

She reached up to a metal switch in the corner, flicked it up, then down, then up and down and up again. Pressing down on the button once more, she licked her lips, trying to gather strength in her lost voice.

"Saluton. This is... Hemera. Hemera Nyx." She licked her lips again, trying to clear her throat. It felt like the first time she'd said her name out loud. "I'm in the..."

She looked around, running her naked hands smoothly across the top of the consoles and monitors. A block of text filled the forward monitor's screen:

```
            ======
      [ROYAL UNITED INDUSTRIES]
            ======
        [LOG: ANK-12519-C]
      [CLASS: SPARROW 1-SEAT]
   [HOMESHIP: IMPERION KONKERO]
            ======
    [CIN: G-FN-RA-12-9799-5]
       [NAME: HEMERA NYX]
         [STATUS: ESTRO]
        [FORTRESS: NYX]
    [KINGDOM: IMPERION ALIANCO]
            ======
```

Hemera ran her other finger slowly across the text, half-turning back to the radio as she wrinkled her forehead at all the information she didn't understand.

"Uh... in the... *Sparrow*." She released the button. The gentle static was unbroken. She pushed down again.

"Is anybody out there?" The static continued. She pressed down again.

"There's somebody in here." She released the button again, pulling away from the radio. The deep void stretched out endlessly in all sparkling directions. Everything felt so still it was almost as if time itself had frozen, the warmth and light of stars trapped forever in the endless cold.

Leaning down forward on the saddle seat, Hemera folded her uninjured arm under her head and sighed. She could see herself clearly in the reflection of the hatch window, ruddy skin with dark freckles on her cheeks and nose, the thick, curly yellow hair, irises shining almost like they had an inner light. The gentle static continued as a feeling enveloped her, a warming sensation of love, and just for a moment, she felt like she was being gently hugged.

Wrapped in the arms of the unknown, she drifted off to sleep.

```
======= [ALWAYS FORWARD] =======
```

"Aahh!" The startlingly loud alarm almost sounded like a gunshot, and Hemera went from dozing to crystal clear awareness.

```
=======
[!FUEL LOW!]
=======
```

If the alarm sound and color of the displayed warning were as bad as they seemed, she decided it was worth trying to figure out what was going on... and fast. Typing on the keypads next to the front monitor seemed like a safer bet than just pushing buttons at random, so she clicked through various options and screens, trying to find information. It didn't take long to learn how to navigate the different screens, reading each heading, until she found an option that sounded promising:

```
=======
[TRAINING MANUALS]
=======
[FLIGHT OPERATIONS]
[NAVIGATION]
[MAINTENANCE]
[...]
=======
```

She studied it more closely than she'd ever studied anything in her life, even as she plugged an ear against the noise. Soon she had located the main engine controls on the handlebars, and pulled them back to zero. The alarm clicked off, but forward display continued to blaze a bright caution.

```
======
[!WARNING!]
[!FUEL LOW!]
======
```

Next came study. She read and re-read each small guide-screen, following the instructions to the letter. Soon she learned how to read the basic display information. According to her best guess, she'd been accelerating into space since she first left the planet. Now she was very far away, and moving at an astonishing speed.

The electronic operating manual went on, covering each obvious and obscure function of the little spaceship. And with each cautious button press, switch flip, and knob turn, the *Sparrow* became more and more under her control. Hemera continued to read and study, pausing several times to nap, time itself seeming to suspend in the small bright bubble that shot through space.

```
======[COME SAIL AWAY]======
```

Emptied, the final water pouch was tossed aside as Hemera shifted and settled back into the seat with a loud burp. She reflexively covered her mouth and looked around in fear for a moment, concerned someone had heard her, then slapped her hand off her mouth, rebuking herself with her hoarse voice.

"I can burp if I want to. I can *fart* as loudly as I want. Who's going to stop me?" She shifted to the side, then frowned as she found her body didn't have one queued up. She made a mental note to let her butt-trumpet toot freely in celebration now that she was... she was...

Something tightly wound deeply inside loosened as a new sense of relaxation flowed through her. She gently rotated her recovering shoulder, letting the peace of outer space and the joy of escape overtake her.

It wasn't just the escape from the hellish planet. It was an escape from something... blurry, buried in her locked memories. A padded cage with thick golden bars. The doors had been blasted off the hinges. The wild animal known as Hemera Nyx had been unleashed.

She was really *free*. At least, for the moment. The *Sparrow* had saved her life, but unless she could find someone or something, her lifeboat would become a coffin. A frown tugged at the edges of her mouth as she considered the road ahead - by her best guess, it seemed like it would be a long journey to anywhere.

She shifted on the padded saddle seat and tapped at the navigation monitor. It was a glass-plated digital display on which the galaxy itself unfurled before her, a dense maze of square dots with jagged lines.

According to the instructions, putting the *Sparrow* into a 'gravity tunnel' would let her travel vast distances at mind-boggling speeds, and then stopping with nearly impossible precision. But more accurately, she wouldn't actually 'go' anywhere - it was outer space that would go around her. From here to there, while also still here. Or something like that.

And that was the easy part. Since the distances were so vast, even a nearly perfect form of travel was subject to variables. A slight dust cloud, a few pebbles - anything pushing or pulling on the gravity tunnel could drop a spaceship out a crazy distance from where the traveler intended to be. According to the information screens, that's where the 'Lamps' came in. Outposts had layers of those small beacons broadcasting distance and direction. She tapped her forehead. Tunneling seemed like it would be relatively easy. Then she'd had to find a Lamp and learn how to follow the directions, accelerating and slowing at the right times. And then...

The nearest dot on her navigation display was labeled [OUT-POST]. Somewhere in the blank of her memories was the idea that outposts, space stations... that these were not *human* things. Intelligent alien civilizations, thousands or millions of galactic governments, every form of life from every corner of the galaxy, it all waited for her to take a true leap into the unknown.

Hemera rubbed her head again as she turned a knob, zooming the display to her current location. She'd been making a lot of leaps into the unknown lately. She frowned as she tapped the screen with a forced thoughtfulness, trying to use her growing fear as energy.

"Let's do it." Following the instructions on the monitor, Hemera pressed a button, then whispered to herself as she shivered.

"Gravity Chain, set."

The *Sparrow* rotated into place, the weight of a far-distant star locked against the mass of her ship. She frowned, then reached up to a small panel over her head and clicked four red rubber-coated switches. She spoke louder, adopting a grander voice, trying to hold her head up a little more despite the shivering.

"S-stabilizers, *engaged*."

Her wrinkled forehead relaxed as her smile unconsciously grew. Another switch: the shield. It was nothing so powerful as to protect her from weapons, but the shimmery electro-static barrier would prevent her from being exposed to the lethal radiations of deep space.

Second-to-last, a press of a lever to release a metal cover, revealing a thicker, heftier button. She took a deep breath, then pressed. The ship bounced slightly as it disconnected from 'local' space. This was the inside of a gravity tunnel. It just looked like the usual impossibly deep canvas of stars and galaxies, but Hemera could *feel* the difference. Dream-like, a shift in reality itself, it was impossible to describe.

The last thing left to do was push the button, glowing on the console ahead of her. It was larger that most of the others, and clearly labeled 'Start.' Her heart beat hard and fast, her finger hovering just above it as she took one final look outside.

Far away from the crimson star, the void was becoming vividly alive, a nearly solid wall of light, the sparkling multi-colored universe singing in its unrestricted glory. The pain in her shoulder and the rumbling in her stomach told a truth that flowed through her with a warm grin: she was *alive*. She had woken up on that hellhole of a planet with no memories. Injured, hunted, attacked, she'd almost died a hundred times over. But there was something else in her spirit now.

Her own raw voice yelled a challenge into the universe, and her reflection in the glass smiled back at her. It was her reflection, but different - there was something more solid around the eyes now. She had *won*. And not only was she still alive, not only did she escape, she now had her very own spaceship.

She smiled wider at the reflection of small, dark freckles on her cheeks that matched the stars. The tangle of deeply sunset-colored hair that was impossible to manage.

Her hero.

The Start button was ready. Beaming at the undeniable truth of who she now was, Hemera raised her arm up high, finger extended.

"Hemera Nyx, *Space Adventurer*... to the GALAXY!" It seemed kind of silly, but she shoved that feeling aside and shouted with a hoarse voice full of spirit:

"TO *ADVENTURE!*"

She brought her finger down hard, missing the button by a centimeter.

"Ah! Oops," she said as she deliberately pressed the button down.

The edge between reality and fiction blurred as the *Sparrow* crackled, stretched, and vanished into the galaxy.

FILE: THE SECRET HORRORS!
TIME: 12044:01:26:11:46
LOCATION: KONKERO MAINTENANCE SECTOR 4, JUNCTION A-28-D

Six walked two paces behind his daughter and watched as she took in the sights. Her stride was a carbon copy of her mother's: almost offensively confident.

The thinning stream of maintenance workers gave a wide berth as they strode down the bare access corridor. Six was supposed to keep his eyes down in the proper manner of a *negrava* following a *sentima*, but he couldn't help but be awed by his youngest. Her rich, deeply banana-yellow tangle of hair reminded him of sunlight, stirring buried memories of the long-distant Earth.

The steel corridor, brightly lit with exposed gravity bulbs, wasn't as beautiful as the ornate wooden hallways of the Fortress Nyx section. The Nyx children were rarely allowed to leave, so Six imagined that any fresh sight would be welcome, including these dingy, industrial scenes.

The corridor terminated in a rounded equipment room, a set of transparent airlock doors hinting at the massive service tunnel just on the other side. Two workers were finishing up a shift, metal locker doors slamming, the mumbling conversation ending suddenly as the young noblewoman strode in, her commoner father right behind.

She surveyed the room like she owned it. The two men shuffled out, their faces stone, eyes

down. Six could feel the emotions rolling off
them as they spitefully walked by. Their RUI
overalls were a pale, impoverished version of
hers: a richer, deeper blue, trimmed in golden
thread, the embroidered symbol for Fortress Nyx
cutting a shadow across the front.

It would have been an enjoyable afternoon
hanging out with his little troublemaker, but
the side-eyes from the workers stung him like
cold needles. She had made too much trouble this last time. The blame for the event
that rocked the *Konkero* had been placed on her
shoulders. The dust had only recently settled,
and taking her out of the Nyx quarters was
risky from almost every angle.

Six, used to being hated, placed a reassuring hand on his daughter's shoulder, but the
unyielding response told him she didn't want or
need it as she broke away towards the equipment lockers. They prepped in silence. Masks
for air, and a recycler connected to a thick
belt. A work-light. A **RAMA** - hand-held welder
and extensible pry-bar. A powered glove with a
long, curly cord. The stocky propulsion foot-
wear with magnetized-rubber soles that she insisted on calling "rocket boots." And a battery
pack, also connected to the belt, to make it
all work.

Six could work through the safety-check
on muscle memory alone, but given it was his
daughter, he made sure to check each point and
connection twice, but the obvious fact was that
she was set and secure. In a third of the time
since the last time they were down here, too.
Six's grin soured somewhat as they stepped
into the airlock, looking past the glass door
into the dark amalgam of pipes and wiring, the

semi-coherent conduits, pumps, and sundry that kept the people aboard the massive spaceship alive.

The airlock shut and hissed, only needing a second to equalize. The maintenance tunnels had an atmosphere to keep pressurization. This far into the ship, however, the gases were unregulated and possibly lethal to breathe in for too long.

They both jumped off the ledge, breaking free from the final gravity bulb's radiation into a soft float. Six shivered and sighed as a missing warmth flooded his flesh and bones, his body embracing the respite from the endless chill of artificial gravity. His daughter expressed her relief more actively, her boots igniting as she grunted, giggled, and danced, shooting blasts of propulsion like fireworks as she spun and bounced around the empty space.

Her expertise with her boots was obvious, and bad news. Training in secret was one thing, but she wasn't even bothering to hide her skill. Each precise twist and spin was an open defiance of rule and law - not to mention her mother's own wishes.

All the more reason for them to talk.

======

Ahead of them, the service tunnel was a gaping black hole ringed by large metal and glass pipes that curved in and out. The thrumming, whooshing, and occasional gurgling of the thickly layered tubing gave the impression of a deep cave, at the end of which snored an enormous monster.

Six's eyes had already started adjusting, turning the black into a deep abyss of small running lights as he started talking, their work-lights flashing as they boosted and adjusted their way to the handle-tracks.

"The primitive part of our brains tells us that going into a dark cave is a bad idea, but I promise there are no primordial monsters waiting for us down there." He waved his hand at a steel tube, twice as thick as a human, ringed with red and white checkered stripes that bent and curved into the darkness.

"That's our pipe." As they neared the track handles, Six rotated upside-down and smiled. "So our brains are structured for gravity, for up-and-down, right? And when we left the air-lock, this tunnel was, to our view, somewhat *down*, right?"

Six didn't need to see his kid's face to know that she was rolling her eyes with her little sigh, but he pressed on regardless.

"When I first started on the crew, I got a little panicky going into these tunnels. Felt like I was going down forever, like I'd never get back up again." He tapped his head, implying genius. "Then one day I thought, what if instead of 'down,' I went 'up'?"

His daughter let out a burp in her mask, then refuted the idea as she grabbed the handle. "But what if you're afraid of heights?"

Six's curly salt-and-pepper hair pointed into the hole like it was an endless ascension up into the black. He looked down at her, with her sunlight hair pointed down, ready to fly, from his perspective, feet-first upwards.

He smiled. "Ready? One, two…"

They both gave a nod as they engaged the track and began sliding silently into the gloom, the occasional flash of a maintenance light marking their speed, their hair waving wildly.

They traveled in silence for a time. The tunnel widened briefly, pipes shooting out and in as they snaked along, revealing a section of the transparent hull. Behind it, the endless starscape - intensely brilliant this far in space - shone sparkling and jagged from the micro-fractures on the thick metal-infused glass.

Six opened himself to the bright light, hand still firmly gripping the handle. "Ah, sunshine!" He glanced up to see a smile curled around her mouth as she watched him pretended to bathe in it, and he winked.

The tunnel suddenly constricted, the starlight vanishing into darkness, their bright work lights showing the pipes speeding by. His daughter yelled, grabbing the handle with both hands and slamming the brake. Her dad almost lost his grip on the handle as he started laughing and slowing to a quick stop.

"Hey bucket-head, you good?"

The mirth lessened in his face, and he nodded seriously as he motioned for them to continue. She ignored him as she tried to shake off the shock. Six opened his mouth, but his daughter pointed in the direction they were traveling, then shut her eyes and clenched her fist, using her very physical way of trying to think.

He watched, intrigued, as she opened her eyes and snapped her fingers. Pulling herself up on her handle, she shifted perpendicular to the track and shoved a boot under the handle, then nodded, a smile growing on her face.

"It's not up or down. I'm going *forward*!"

Six was struck by the proclamation. The solution was very *her*. She struck a dramatic pose and shifted her foot, speeding up. They continued down the track for exactly twelve seconds before he started talking.

"Well, I guess you know by now that I didn't just bring you out here to find a sewage leak." It caught her by surprise, a fact betrayed by her sealed-off face before she could deny it. Six fought the feeling that she was standing up and he was sliding along the floor as they continued forward.

"Well…" he said, waving his free hand, trying to reestablish his own sense of up. "It's time you learned the secret language."

She blinked as they continued. "The what?"

"The *secret language*. It's the missing piece in your puzzle. Once you get this one figured out, you'll be unstoppable."

She nodded. Then she nodded again. Then looked at him through their visors, dim lights reflecting lines across the glass.

"So what… is that?"

"*Subtlety!*" He snapped his fingers. "You need to see how other people have been using it against you." He paused, then shrugged. "And, maybe even learn how to use it for yourself."

The sour look on her face was a verbal an answer as any spoken aloud. Six felt a tug of anger in his chest. It was his fault for the humor, but she was not taking this seriously.

"I'm serious. What I'm going to tell you is more important than your… *incident*. You *need* to start paying more attention."

The incident had affected her more deeply than she cared to admit, although her stone face was as strong a response as yelling for help. He had touched a raw nerve, but this was no time to be subtle.

"Let's check the offset-pipe here," he said, bringing them both to a standstill near a smaller dark hole, bending off somewhere deeper in. They gently boosted themselves to the rim and looked in.

They were very deep in the ship. Shining her work light down the endless, gently curving tunnel with trepidation, she spoke first.

"I heard there were man-eating monsters living in the tunnels," she whispered, her eyes following the curves and shadows with her light. "That's why people keep going missing."

Six motioned for her to sit, or close enough in the absent gravity, while he anchored himself on a nearby utility box. The wind fluttered his floating hair as he looked deeply in every

direction. Nodding, he turned back to her with
an unusual intensity.

"Hemera Nyx."

=======

Six hoped she felt the full weight of it, him
using her adult name. It was technically il-
legal for him to call her 'Nyx' until she was
recognized in her own time, but what they were
about to discuss required Hemera to act like an
adult.

It seemed a good way to start. Hemera adjusted her position, sitting up a little straighter
in a young teenager's imitation of a respectable adult. Her hair had spread in all directions in the zero gravity, giving her something
akin to a fuzzy halo.

"That's bold, dad. I could report you."

Six leaned back against the wall, found it
uncomfortable, then crouched as he replied.
"We can talk freely, 'mera, but we can't stay
long, and I have a *lot* to tell you, so listen.
There's no easy way to say this, so I'm just
going to lay it out: *we are still in danger.*"

He paused to make sure he had her full attention. "Real, life-and-death danger. And this…
it's not your fault. Listen. Everyone knows
that kid was a bully, you were right to stand
up to him. But didn't you think the protests
were out of proportion for a child's broken
nose?"

Hemera's eyes turned to the same glassy sheen
as her visor as numbers rolled off her tongue,

memorized, internalized. "Two hundred seventy-four injured. Eighty-six missing. Twelve dead."

Six reached out and grabbed her shoulder, giving her a shake. "You know how I know it's not your fault? *Listen*." He leaned closer. "There was an *organization* to it. Do you understand?"

His hand gestured wildly. "Specific individuals were… targeted. Infrastructure junctions were hijacked. Security checkpoints hit with prototype weapons, weapons stolen directly from the Labs. You see? This wasn't some random riot. Gods-hell, our navi…"

He shook his head, breaking eye contact, but Hemera cocked her head. "What's wrong with the navigation?"

"Nothing. Listen. All of that at the *exact* same time as the riots. You think a punch caused all that? It was *planned*. Idiots. Bastard *idiots*. Hemera!" His drifted eyes snapped back to hers. "Where do you think we are right now?"

"Konkero maintenance sector four, junction A-"

"WE'RE IN OUTER SPACE!" The yell escaped his lips as the shout echoed oddly up and down the curving tunnels. He hushed himself, then motioned for them to hide a little farther back.

"Can you just please tell me what's going on?" Hemera's confusion was giving into a panic. Six's eyes grew more serious as he pointed outside. Outside the ship was in every direction, his finger jumping around to make that point clear.

"We. Are. In. Outer. Space. The *void*." He gestured to the stars, hidden behind the curtain of pipes and tubing. "The void is death, Hemera. The *Konkero* is *surrounded* by it. And if these machines break down, if the hull breaks, *if we fight each other*, then death will be *inside* the *Konkero*, too. Do you understand? No injuries, no missing, just *forty thousand dead people*."

Six snapped back from his rant at the sight of Hemera's wide, watery eyes behind her mask. He released his grip on her arms and waved at the dark tunnels in front and behind, trying to hold on to a pipe to keep from drifting away.

"There *are* monsters on this ship: an organized group of people who are doing everything in their power to kill everyone aboard. They are making progress on their goal right now, as we speak, and the Reganto has no way of fighting back without giving them everything they're asking for. Do you understand, Hemera? It's not just angry negrava or incompetent sentima. There are people aboard who are actively sabotaging the ship. They're trying to kill us. *All* of us."

Hemera managed the stiffest of nods, her brown-green eyes even wider.

"Your mom didn't want me to tell you all of this. But I see you - you're a young lady now, aren't you? You threw that punch to protect someone else, didn't you?" He didn't wait for an answer. "That's not what a *child* does, right? So, welcome to -."

The tunnel flashed as a bright light flew up from deeper in. A shadow sped by, somewhat distant on the other side of the tunnel. Hemera heard the grinding of the brake, then the quick reversal, the stranger shining his work light on both of them as he reappeared.

"Saluton?" The stranger spoke loudly over the whooshing and gurgling in the tunnel as he flicked his light back and forth, getting a good view of both of them.

"Saluton!" Six jumped up and motioned to Hemera. "We're on the hunt for a sewage leak," he said, pointing to the pipe they had been following.

"What's the work order?"

Six didn't miss a beat. "No work order. We're here on the Commands, Eduction Section Three. On-site training for potential Fortress heirs." He gestured to Hemera. "You know?"

They couldn't see the man, hidden as he was on the far side behind his work light, which now trained on Hemera as if he was seeing her for the first time. The reflections off her overall's embroidery showered the tunnel with thin bands of golden light.

"Ah. *Nyx*. And you're Six?"

Six smiled and shook Hemera's shoulder lightly. "Estro Nyx insists *her* children learn every facet of the *Konkero's*…"

"Yeah, I get it," the man said, clicking off his light, becoming nothing more than a dark, human-shaped outline. He began to ascend, then stopped to look back at them. "The Reganto is giving a speech in a half-hour. It's our duty to watch it."

"*Gloro de Servo*," said Six as he and Hemera saluted, right hands touching their heads, then their left shoulders. Seemingly satisfied, the man vanished back into the tunnel, the darkness following swiftly behind.

Six turned back to his child, so far as she was still was one. The harsh sunlight of adulthood was burning away the fog of innocence. He imagined only a few days of childhood remained in her.

"I'm sorry," he said, "that was my fault. You did well, bucket-head." He nodded at her with relief.

"Why does it matter? Why are you telling me all of this? What the gods-hell am I supposed to do?" Hemera staggered, then dropped into the zero gravity, hands on her sides of her face as she floated and whined. Six watched her speak, now more to herself than to him.

"I don't have any power. I'm just going to be a prisoner of Fortress Nyx until the negrava rise up and kill us all."

Hemera looked him right in the eyes, realizing what she was saying as it escaped her mouth. "I'm sorry, dad. I just…"

Six nodded solemnly, trying to take a closer seat to her. "You're right. The world is stacked against you. Nearly everyone - negrava and sentima alike - want you dead. It's you against the galaxy."

He watched her float, curled up in a ball, buried into herself.

He smiled. "But so what? I've been living that life since the moment I met your mother. People have killed each other, just because I… because your mom and I love each other."

Hemera peeked an eye at her dad as he continued. "Can you imagine? I live it every day - no one can accept me as one of their own. No one but you, your brother, your sister. Your mom. You guys are the only people I have in the…" he paused, then waved to the stars resting in dark, "…in the entire universe."

Hemera had loosened herself from her own grip. Six saw a different light in her eyes, and for a moment he wondered if she had never thought about it before: the repercussions of the choice her mother made when she married a commoner. He wondered if they had ever told her the full story of how Lenna got the scars on her face.

Six nodded as Hemera continued uncurling. "But the real question is…" He smiled at her, giving her the line he'd been using since she was a toddler: "What's slowing you down, kid?"

A half-smile grew behind her glass visor as he continued. "The universe conspires to put you in a cage, to kill you. What are you going to *do* about it?"

Hemera had unfurled and now floated thoughtfully as Six leaned in.

"An even better question is: What are your commands, *Estro?*" He smiled widely, then covered the distance to shuffle her hair and tapped the top of her visor with his. "We should get moving."

======

They were moving farther into the tunnel. Hemera shook her head as they traveled, a statement of reality against the question.

"I'm not going to be Estro. Dee is."

Six's smile faded as he spoke over the rushing air. "I know you've heard Defiant making a point of not wanting it, as he does so often and loudly at the dinner table."

"Mom says she said the same thing when she was his age, that he'll take his responsibility when the time comes."

Six's teeth grit a bit. "*Subtlety,* dummy. Think wider! Outside the family, who gains the most if Fortress Nyx breaks? Defiant has a role to play in keeping our home together - in keeping this ship operational. But we can't *make* him take it. When the time really comes… we all know what his choice is."

Six couldn't help the tug of sadness on his throat at the statement. He could never be a Nyx, but nature had bypassed his childhood servant-surgeries and given him three miracles in the form of children - and a fourth child, adopted but equally loved, named *Fortress Nyx.*

Hemera's gears were turning. "Then Star. She's older than me. She can be in her own time if…"

They continued to speed along the track, Six projecting his more emotional voice to be heard. "Starandria is going to change her mind? You know she *chose* to not be recognized, right? She is a brilliant scientist, but she… well, she can hardly leave her lab these days."

Six's love and worry for his daughter pulled at his chest as he weighed the lives at stake. "Do you really think Star is the right choice to stand before the Reganto and push back? To stand in front of ten thousand people and make commands? Star is where she needs to be, doing what she needs to do."

Tapping his knuckle against the glass of his mask, he continued. "Your mom agrees. It would be ineffective and cruel to force Starandria into it. Defiant won't take it. So that leaves… *you*."

They traveled in silence for a time, the endless rush of pipes, cables, and structural struts a blur.

The question left Hemera's mouth like a baby bird. "If I become Estro…" she paused, feeling the weight, readjusting her body to carry whatever answers would come. "When I'm Estro, I can tip the vote… I can vote to return to the Earth. Right?"

Six hesitated. "You'll… be able to do everything an Estro can do. Maybe more, given that we're deep in outer space. But it's not as simple as that, 'mera." He let his eyes drift down the seemingly endless tunnels.

"If you think you can overcome cultural pro-
gramming, radically restructure social power, bring peace and happiness to the passengers while placating whomever is in charge, all
without getting a weapon shoved to your head,
then… maybe we can turn around and try to find a
way back to the Earth, yeah."

That seemed to seal the deal. Hemera gave a
thumbs up, the wind buffeting her hair as they
sped along the track.

"Then… leave it to me!"

"Huh." Six couldn't dislike it. He wondered
what he had expected - some sort of push back
perhaps, or a wailing at fate, a passionate re-
jection.

But when Hemera had her spirits up, it was
difficult to stand in her way. Now that she found
a way to turn the *Konkero* around, Hemera seemed
fixated. Six could almost see the sparkling blue
and white orb in the reflection of her eyes.

And then he felt a preemptive sadness for
Hemera when she would find out how much paper-
work the job involved. "Well, your willingness
to…"

He stopped talking as he realized Hemera suddenly wasn't there.

======

Her outline had paused near an opening, like
the one they had passed on their way in, staring out past the hull into the fractured starscape beyond. It took him a moment to flip and
return, slowly pulling up besides.

Her eyes were locked on something outside the hull with absolute intensity. Six followed her gaze and fully gasped.

The vessel outside was unlike anything he'd ever seen: a mechanical… *sea urchin*, a spherical core surrounded by long metal spike-like tubes. Six was dumbstruck as he watched the in- human spaceship spin and float, shining a light from one spike along the hull as it approached, flashing them as it slowly drifted by.

A growing sense of urgency tugged at him, but he couldn't get his brain to work, the words dribbling out. "Is that… what…"

"There's more!" Hemera pointed through the roughed glass at two more alien craft as they streaked past, heading towards the front of the *Konkero*. Six's mind snapped back to reality as the urchin floated farther down the hull.

"We need t-"

Another spike flared to life, firing a bril- liant, wiggling beam of electricity. A mut- ed boom shook down the tunnel as distant glass panels shattered into a sparkling cloud, the living beam carving a path up and down the side of the *Konkero*.

The tunnel lit up in an emergency red as in- structions blared from every speaker. The sound echoed up and down the tunnels in a mad gib- berish. Six grabbed his daughter's hand and snapped on the handle, speeding as fast as he could, the tunnel groaning like a great wounded beast.

"ARE WE BEING ATTACKED BY ALIENS?!" Hemera yelled over the cacophony. Six didn't look back as he swore the longest string of choice words, each new rumble and impact ripping away at the faint shreds of hope he clung to.

They were nearing the entrance. He turned back to look at Hemera, who was keeping her composure better than he was. He yelled, trying his best to reassure her.

"FUCK!"

Out of fuel and near death, our hero speeds
helplessly through the endless void! Will she
be rescued in time? And what *new* dangers lurk
in the dark?

SPACE ADVENTURER

In...

The Alien Galaxy!

======
[TIME: 12047:07:19:01:02]
======
[LOCATION: OFF-COURSE BY 98208 KM]
======

[STATUS: DYING]

======

=====[LOST AND FOUND]======

The floating body was a shadow outlined by a single warning, the light from the display an ember in the dark, cold cockpit.

======

[!WARNING!]
[!FUEL DEPLETED!]

======

Water had run out fifty hours ago. Food, more than a hundred. She had escaped hell and passed out with the primary engine burning through her fuel, pushing her faster and faster into the void. Tunneling hadn't been an issue, but her momentum was too great, and her fuel reserves too low, to adjust her course upon arrival.

Beeping. Flashing.

The pain in her throat was unbearable, the dull ache squeezed at her body. The dry, sticky haze of her mind danced around the single law of physics: something in motion remains so.

Strong organic vocalizations, a commanding sort of gibberish.

There wasn't much to be aware of in those increasingly rare moments of lucidity. She had flown past the second Lamp significantly off-course, and then the third bubble of small transmitters flew by. The small devices broadcasting the location of the Outpost that she would never reach called out for her as she helplessly flew deeper into the nothing. The course was set; the Void waited for her.

The Sparrow *shuddered for a moment. Then it shook, rocking back and forth.*

She had even tried pushing the *Sparrow* with her rocket boots. While they were incredible at moving her around, they lacked the power to shove her ship enough to gain the right trajectory. Her rough calculations of boot-thrust against velocity put it near two hundred years of constant pushing just to turn around.

Squeaking, grinding, the sound of metal on metal, the feeling of slowing as her body drifted forward, thudding against the glass.

The radio console was beeping.

Hemera opened her sticky eyelids, trying to focus. Something was *different*. A flash outside the cockpit; the flare of a ship's engines. Several points of fuzzy light sped around as the *Sparrow* shook again.

Her brain started whirring, starting up processes long shut as something began scrolling across the radio's translation display. She had difficulty getting her eyes to focus as the bright symbols rolled across.

[??? ??? *????*]

Her body felt like thick putty, but she kicked and swam to the gravity control and fell to the ground with a hard thump. Crawling with sparks at the edges of her vision, she made it to the radio console, arms shaking and weak.

"H-hello? Saluton..." she coughed, dry throat and cracked lips objecting to use. "Do you have... any water?"

She tried to hold her head as it throbbed in pain, the terror of hallucinations barking at the edges. The reply came marching across the screen with an electronic clicking and grumbling.

[??? GIVE/DONATE ??? WE/US *????*]

"I... don't..." she looked around the cramped cockpit, barely enough room for her among the consoles and saddle-seat. She turned back to the radio, a single clear thought coming through her hard throat.

"Whatever I have, it's yours. Take the ship... take everything. Please. I just... I... just want to live."

[AERONAUT/PILOT ???/??? ??? DEMANDS *COMMAND*]

The lights outside spun around the ship, until one bright light flooded the chamber, blinding her, her skull an empty vessel.

[??? SPECIES. ??? *CAUTION*]

[???/??? VOID/SPACE PROTECTION/EQUIPMENT ???/ EGRESS ???/PROMISED CONFIRM/??? *COMMAND*]

She smacked her dry, cracked lips, trying to summon enough moisture to speak, voice weak and cracking. "Confirm."

Putting her spacesuit on made sense. She began the longest, most agonizing effort of putting her suit on, her muscles and brain made of mud, disappointed in herself for not leaving it on. Suit on and helmet secured, Hemera extracted her **PLOT**. The ship shut down for the first time since she initially started it on that hellish planet, so very far away. Pulling on the cockpit handle with the last of her strength, she was shocked by the alien hands that reached in and yanked her out into space with the burst of escaping air.

She spun for a moment, only to be caught by powerful arms and held in check, the streaking lines vibrating back to dots as she looked back at the *Sparrow*.

Odd alien spacesuits were swarming her spaceship. Stubby legs kicked as one searched the cockpit, while what seemed to be a transparent glowing blob wormed its way around one of the wings. Five more floated underneath, poking and prodding. The bright flash of a welding torch marked the union of spaceship to hauling chain.

There was more, just beyond. Spaceships. Long, curved ones. Stubby boxes bristling with guns. And other shapes that seemed almost nonsense. The fear of hallucinations cracked deeper into her mind.

While she tried to make sense of it all, strong appendages poked and prodded her, feeling the body under her suit, checking the pouches. And then a sudden twirl.

Hemera was face-to-face with her first intelligent, space-faring alien. Four independent stalks stuck out of its visor, each glass protrusion containing a wet, orbed eye. It had a smooth, long face behind its helmet's glass, tapering into a round, worm-like mouth, ringed with small feelers.

The mouth moved, snapping and drooling a bit, as words scrolled in Hemera's helmet. The alien shook her back and forth vigorously. She could barely read, consciousness slipping back and forth as she wiggled around in space.

[??? ??? HEALTHY/??? RESPOND *CONCERN*]

"Nuuuhhhh..." she breathed. "I'm... so... thirsty."

The worm-like alien stopped shaking and drew her closer, pressing its visor to hers. She could see the slime on its brown-pinkish skin, the deep pores expanding and contracting like lungs.

[??? BIOLOGICAL ???/NEEDS *????*]

Her heart beat hard in the intelligent alien's four-eyed stare. "Wha... water. H... h two oh. Hydrogen... dioxide..."

A unknown voice filled her helmet, a hard clicking and whistling, contrasting with the warm murmuring of the alien worm-man.

[???/NO ???/??? LOST ???/PILOT. RECRUIT ??? *ASSESSMENT*]

The wormy alien burbled in response, the translation coming through her helmet's display.

[??? ??? HANDLE/NAME ??? *QUESTION*]

She took a deep breath as her eyes began to roll back into her head.

"Hemera... Nyx..."

The wormy one smiled, showing a perfectly circular ring of small blue teeth.

[HEMERA NYX. WATER/LIQUID ??? FOOD/??? ???.
WELCOME/JOINED ??? FANGS OF/THE VOID. *CONGRAT-
ULATIONS*]

The last word scrolled across her visor as everything faded to black.

====== [THE WORM] ======

"HACK! BLEGH!"

Hemera woke up spitting up gulps of water, sputtering and wheezing. Her desperate hands grasped and pulled the tube out from deep inside her throat, but it was too late to twist, her body too sluggish to avoid vomiting phlegmy water all over itself as the tube came out. Her heavy head thudded back on the padded shelf as the small metal room spun for a moment, the water seeping back into the dried cracks of her mind. She took a deep, shuddering breath. And then another. And again, until the rhythm settled.

"I'm still alive."

A chuckle of relief escaped her chapped lips, followed by another, and then another. Her laughter turned hysteric, crossing the line into a wild sobbing as the profound relief filled her limbs with water.

The sobbing faded quickly as a chill brushed against her back. Wiping her nose with a naked hand, Hemera scanned the elongated cube-like room. The light was a pleasing shade of light yellow, but the color was at odds with the cold air circulating around her. The hard rest-shelf under her was uncomfortable, but the mild curve of its lines matched the room, giving it a homey sort of feel. There was a heap of pointed boots and thin gloves in one corner, near what seemed to be a large sliding door.

At the opposite end was a wall of switches and knobs pocked with a few simple displays. Her clearing vision traced the outline of her life-support pack connected to the wall by tubes and cables, then focused on a familiar handle sticking out of the console.

Unsteady, Hemera plodded over, the freezing floor shocking her naked feet. Her skin prickled, her senses sharpening as cold air seeped into her flesh, suddenly aware of the frigid air flowing in through small vents in the ceiling. Shivering, she wrapped her arms around her as she made her way forward. Taking a long, thoughtful glug from the still-running water hose in her hand, she scanned the wall with thoughtful curiosity. A few switches clicked up and down, then she wiggled a few knobs.

Nothing happened.

Shrugging, Hemera grabbed her **PLOT**'s handle and twisted. The lights in the pod dimmed; the air stilled. She twisted it back. The lights brightened, the breeze rushed back.

"Hmm…" she grumbled, looking up at her life support pack. She had just began wondering where her spacesuit had gone when a rustling and mumbling sound made her jump back into the corner, heart about to burst in fright.

The heap in the corner was standing up.

Fully upright, it began to shake. Four wiggly arms sprung from the slightly bronze spacesuit and quickly grew longer. The burbling murmur sounds grew louder as the figure took a wobbly step on a bendy leg towards her, four arms stretched wide. Hemera stood stock-still, her impossibly wide eyes locked on the figure. It paused, arms still in the air, then bent forward for a moment before wiggling back upright, flicking a small switch on its long, curved helmet. From the console, a tinny, robotic voice spoke.

[APOLOGIES/FORGIVENESS. ???/ENTITY ???/???
TRANSLATOR/PLOT/TALK *????*]

Hemera's eyes darted back and forth between the console and the creature, who slowly lowered its arms, then gently sat on the vacant resting shelf.

[YOU/ENTITY ARE/??? ALIVE/EXIST. THIS/STATUS ??? GOOD/ACCEPTABLE. *RELIEF*]

She could see the slimy worm-face through the elongated glass visor, the four eyestalks watching her.

"...*Leoborah's tits*. You're an *alien*. A *real* alien..."

Her new hydration had already worked its way through her skin, sweat drenching her forehead despite the cold air.

"...*holy shit*."

She began shivering, then looked back at the console as a flow of noises matched with the alien murmuring, one arm tapping the side of its helmet.

[OUR/??? TRANSLATION/SELECTION REQUIRES/NEEDS WORK/??? *ASSESSMENT*]

There was a tugging in her chest, and through Hemera's panic she felt an instinctive urge to do what a real space adventurer would do: say hello.

"*Hel... saluton*. Uh... my name is Hemera. Hemera Nyx. I... come in peace." She flashed a peace sign with her hand, then wrapped it back around her as she swallowed hard. "I'm... it's... nice to meet you, mister... alien. Sir? Or not! ...*shit!*"

The bronze-suited creature gave a slow sort of nod than gradually turned into an informal bow, like some sort of gelatinous dessert bending in a dainty silver spoon.

[I/ME HAVE ???/GREETED YOU/HEMERA NYX *ASSUR-ANCE*]

"Ah...?" The memory of her rescue came back to her - it was the same alien as before, the one who had grabbed her as she was flung free of the *Sparrow*. Her arms still wrapped around herself, trying to keep the heat in as she gulped more water, suddenly worried about her spaceship.

"I'm sorry, I've... been through a lot, and... my memory... my brains aren't..." She shook her head again as she jumped up and down. "I'm sorry, can we... I'm *freezing!*"

At this the wormy alien rose from its seat in a smooth motion, launching into a surprisingly graceful amble to the wall of switches and knobs next to her. Hemera saw the strong bend and flex of legs and realized that this creature probably did not have any bones.

[DOES/IS HEMERA NYX UNFAMILIAR/??? REST-POD/??? OPERATIONS *QUESTION*]

Hemera continued to press herself into the corner as the alien clicked a switch, then slowly turned a knob. Warm air flowed quickly in as the alien turned to look at her, still rotating the knob.

"Ah... that's... right *there*." Warmth flooded her veins as she hesitantly stepped out, breathing deeper. "Oh, thank the *gods...*"

Her arms dropped to her sides as the hot prickles began working their way back in to her fingers and toes, the breeze whooshing warmth into the room. The wormy one leaned against the console, wrapping its four arms around themselves, watching. Hemera caught a glimpse of a **PLOT** device along the creature's hip.

"...thank you. Thank you," Hemera said again, the gratitude suddenly spilling out. "Thank you!"

She opened her arms wide, spun into a tight cartwheel, then threw a celebratory fist into the air.

"I'm freaking ALIVE!"

The celebration proved too much for her recovering body to handle. Her head spun as her butt landed hard on the cold steel floor. 'Wormy' stepped forward, surprised at the sudden outburst.

[I/THIS PLEASED/DELIGHTED ??? ??? *STATEMENT*
CAUTION FOR/WITH RECOVERY/HEALING *CONCERN*]

The ecstasy of being alive faded quickly into the reality that, in every way, shape, and form, she was at this alien's mercy. Hemera shifted to a knee, hoping that formally lowering herself was something universally acknowledged, but the wormy alien jumped itself stiffly upright and waved it's wiggly arms threateningly, a hard edge to the loud murmurs.

[YOU/HEMERA NYX HAVE INSULTED ME/I GRIEVOUSLY/
SERIOUSLY *OUTRAGE*]

Hemera's blood froze. "I'm-I'm-I'm s-s-sorry!"

The creature leaned over her, giving her a death stare from those independent stalks. It suddenly made a hard barking noise as it leaned back, still honking and wet coughing, little blue teeth clacking together.

[*HUMOR*]

Hemera tilted her head at the audio translation as she watched the jiggling body.

Wormy was *laughing*.

A casual, wiggly, space-suited arm patted the top of her head as the alien moved past her and headed towards the door. Then it checked its arm, wiped it against its bodysuit, and then waved a different arm at Hemera's suit roughly shoved under the rest shelf.

[USE/INHABIT VOID/SPACE SUIT/SAFETY *SUGGES-
TION*]

The skintight suit and mechanical supports snapped on quickly. It was a struggle to disconnect the hoses and cables from her life support pack, but it only took a moment more before the final click of the second helmet latch. The rubber neck-piece inflated as the pressurization kicked in, giving her the brief sensation of being choked.

"Gah, *hack*, grrr..." Hemera said, trying in vain to loosen the inflated rubber. Wormy stood next to the door, regarding her. She could imagine a kind of bemused expression on the strange alien face, interested in the odd stranger it had saved from the endless nothing.

Hemera walked up besides, exhausted, starving, but filled to the brim with excitement.

"You know, you remind me of someone." She looked the alien right in the stalks, well past any lingering fears she had. This one alien was kind enough to save her life, and that meant kindness wasn't just limited to humans. Hope was growing in her chest. "He was..."

Hemera gaped for a moment, suddenly aware of her lack of memories. Whoever he had been, this creature reminded her of him. She shook her head, giving her helmet a knock.

"Actually, never mind. Wormy - ah, sorry, is that OK? That's not an insult to call you that, is it? What is your name, anyway? How do names work out here? And why do *you* have a **PLOT** device? Who..."

Wormy regarded her for a moment more, then turned to press a button near the doors, his murmuring scrolling across her bottom display.

[HAVE/NEED LEARN MUCH/MANY, HEMERA NYX. *STATE-MENT*]

The interior of the room exploded into foam, the rainbow suds filling the space completely. Hemera watched, delighted, as the bubbles gathered everywhere she had touched. Hissing and steaming, it eradicated any viable forms of life into dust and smoke, then vanished so quickly it was as if they had never been there. The room depressurized, a shockingly loud hiss screeching into silence. Hemera caught her breath as the door slid open, showing a scene directly out and into the void.

"Oh, *wow*..."

They stepped out on a grated walkway and into a small fleet of multicolored spaceships. A pair of sleek vessels, each a long curved line that tapered into rotating engines, decorated with stenciled figures of stylized faces, animals, and various kinds of sloppily painted script covering more formal-looking symbols. A boxy spaceship jetted by, keeping its orientation stable using a multitude of jets and engines stationed on the sides, jumping and shifting with mechanical precision. Another spaceship drifted into view, much closer than the last, and covered with more rough alien scrawls in white and red, the shape of a tube with a large engine at either end, pimples of glass orbs speckling across the surface. These and more weaved and spun, a flock of slow-moving fire birds migrating through vast nothing, piloted by a menagerie of jarringly different lifeforms held together by the absence of all things around them.

Wormy regarded Hemera's slack jaw with amusement.

```
[WELCOME TO THE FANGS/TEETH OF THE VOID/SPACE,
HEMERA NYX.  *GREETING*]


======[SIX MONTHS LATER]======
```

"Too slow, *Sentry*!"

Hemera Nyx threw the tail of the *Sparrow* up as her two towing-claws caught the rim of the blocky spaceship. Her momentum pulled the *Sparrow* into a tight curve, the springy steel cables tugging the larger spaceship around with her.

At the apex of the curve, Hemera pushed her thrusters and flung the *Sentry* into a rapid spin towards their base of operations. The cables quickly reeled in as she disengaged the towing-claws. The *Sentry* flared boosters and stabilizers as her radio filled with insulting alien hoots and honks from the dizzy crew. Hemera didn't bother to respond as she looked for more stragglers, her eyes tracing the thick reinforcements of the block-shaped homeship.

The *Hideout*.

It was an old long-distance dump truck hauler that planet-ripping operations used to transport raw minerals and nearly crossed the line between 'enormous spaceship' and 'tiny spaceport.' The color of dented metal panels that may have once been dark green and yellow covered the surface, while rough welding jobs of steel and iron shone in the bright, deep-space sky. It was ugly, mostly broken, and her home. Hemera felt a warmth in her chest at the metallic patchwork repairs and 'improvements' clearly made by amateurs, herself included.

The *Sentry* finally stopped spinning and lined up behind the rest of the Fangs as they gently entered the cramped bay doors. The rest of the fleet was already locked inside: the tan and green *Striker Eureka*, the deep blue and gentle curves of *Mother's Embrace*, and the half-dozen others, all nestled into their personal anchor points, all grumbling with various complaints.

While any given spaceship could use a gravity tunnel, the vast distances those tunnels covered amplified micro-variations, resulting in an incontrollable level of variation. If the fleet had tried to tunnel to the same location individually, they would have spent the next week trying to find each other - and that's if they were lucky. That fact, however, hardly outweighed the annoyance of those freedom-embracing creatures being shoved and locked into an old cargo hold.

The Fangs had accepted Hemera without question. None of them had ever seen a human before. She was an real alien among aliens, but she was one of them, perhaps even before she was rescued: like the rest, an exile from her own people, alone in the infinite nothing.

Hemera spun the *Sparrow* in a slow circle, glad for the weight of her responsibilities. She knew she still had a lot to learn, so the very least she could do was the job assigned to her by the Leader. Seeing no errant Fang ships to shepherd, her vision flowed out into the void, still in awe of it all: the star-thick nothing they flew on, far from any Outposts or suns, sparkled with the colors of the cosmos; bright reds and blues of galaxies filling the space between the whites, yellows, blues, and all other colored stars. The universe was alive in every spectrometric vibration.

She slapped her helmet to engage the straw, her throat suddenly dry. Tugging thoughtfully at the thin trickle of water recycled by her spacesuit (a function she had only recently discovered, much to her embarrassment), she squared with the fact that the void still scared her - and how close she had come to dying out here. As beautiful as the universe was, it was simply too unforgiving, too *big*, to traverse without the cooperation of many others, all of whom had to look out for each other.

Or so Wormy had said. Hemera had no reason to doubt him, or any of his instructions on how the galaxy works. He had repeatedly warned her about those those possessed of the means and motivation to enslave others: civilizations were rabid beasts built on violence, extraction, and exploitation; they fought endlessly for every star system, for every centimeter of the void still rich enough to feed their infinite appetites.

Then there were the rest, living in the skeletal ruins left by civilized society. She had seen it herself over the past few months - flotillas, caravans, loose groups of outcasts; they skulked at the edges of the more civilized space, building unlisted Outposts from the wreckage of long-forgotten battles, building 'bubble homes' on toxic, strip-minded planets.

Their lack of formal recognition and somewhat fluid morality made the civilized galaxy distrust these groups. Worse, that distrust often existed between caravans as well. Fortunately, the somewhat underground nature of their existence lent itself to certain employment opportunities. Hemera clicked the noise of her radio off as she sped past the closing cargo doors, glad to be rid of their latest 'sealed, don't ask questions' shipment, recently dropped off at a Random Void Location and tagged with a small broadcast tracker for whomever was going to pick it up.

Random Void Locations were just that, wholly arbitrary locations within the vastness of outer space. The odds of randomly finding anything in the endless nothing was less than a rounding error, so having cargo resting in an RVL was, in theory, as secure as physically possible: no one could ever find it without knowing *exactly* where it was.

The translucent half-sphere on the top of the *Hideout* sparkled in the starlight as Hemera sped towards it, and soon she could see figures moving behind the glass. She gave them a good buzz before pulling around underneath, pointed towards the smaller bridge hanger.

The *Sparrow* bent around, primary engine pointed and flaring towards the ship as she slid past the open bridge-hanger door at an alarming speed. A thick gravity web caught her spaceship, immediately slowing to a standstill as her landing claws grabbed the anchor points.

Hemera jumped out of the hatch and blasted her rocket boots, covering the distance to the hallway opening in an instant. She sprinted down a short, dilapidated hallway, the large primary command bridge doors straight ahead as the gravity bulbs tried to match her pace. Cutting a hard left towards the empty elevator shaft, she almost slammed into a alien that looked like a grub in a transparent trash bag. Dozens of tiny prehensile legs wiggled in alarm and annoyance as Hemera spun around it, yelling as she kept her speed.

"Yah! Sorry, Grubby!" The grub farted and shifted color to pink as Hemera jumped into the empty elevator shaft, blasting her boots once more. She sped upwards, then shifted out of the stuck-open door at the top and launching herself out at the top of the glass dome and into a free fall.

She fell into the large, open central command bridge. With a last blast of her boots, she landed calmly in her assigned position. A simple announce-bot woke up, chirping what everyone else had just observed.

[!ATTENTION: SUB-LEADER HEMERA NYX IS NOW ON THE BRIDGE!]

The command bridge of the *Hideout* gave an unrestricted view of half of the sky, as well as four thruster-pointed corners of the monstrous cube. It was a relatively small space given the size of the spaceship, but mineral haulers never required much by way of crew - if any at all, given a handful of cheap robots could handle everything but the most unexpected events.

Wormy swiveled in his central command chair, murmuring loudly.

[HEMERA NYX. *REBUKE*]

======= [LEADER] =======

Hemera bowed. "Leader."

The central command chair sat at the apex of a small steel hill, ringed in station-levels that spread outward to the large windows aflame with stars. Wormy wiggled an arm at her, pointing and shaking it in emphasis.

[RECKLESSNESS AGAIN. SAFETY SHOULD BE MOST ON YOUR MIND AND SPIRIT, NYX. OUR NEXT TUNNEL WILL PUT US WITHIN COLLECTED ALLIANCE SPACE. *LECTURE*]

Hemera's eyes rolled as her visor darkened. Looking out into the sea of light, she remembered when her **PLOT** struggled to translate his low rumbling. She stood impatiently on the second rung, sharing the Leader's view of the terminals. Each station had two displays: one for the crew member who looked up at the Leader, and one for the Leader who looked back down on them. Thick green vines wrapped supports and snaked along the edges, a previous occupant's hobby garden gone wild. Hemera groused as she touched a small orange flower poking up around the edge of the rung.

"You guys all seem scared of this Collective Alliance. Why would they be interested in us? Caravans like ours fly through all the time, right?"

A pile of pipes, hoses, and steel struts stirred close to the glass near the fourth rung, a mechanical mouth clacking and wheezing.

[CARAVAN IS NOT THE ISSUE. *RESENTMENT*]

The objection came from the Energy Distribution Leader, a sentient fungus that lived in a glass tank. Its thin mycelium ran in pipes and hoses that connected to small motors, operating robotic arms, legs, and an assortment of other robotic equipment besides.

Hemera wondered if 'Mushroom' had made itself look like a pile of trash on purpose. It blended right in to the vacant spaces from where an old terminal had once been. It grumbled over its metal shoulder as it turned an optical sensor towards Wormy, who sat upright as he wiggled his head in a commanding fashion.

[SUFFICIENT ON THIS SUBJECT. *COMMAND* SUB-LEADER, WHAT IS OUR READINESS FOR TUNNEL-ING? *REQUEST*]

Hemera twisted her helmet's radio knob to the bridge frequency as she felt the bone-wiggling thud of the cargo doors slamming shut. It rattled the structural frame of the *Hideout* as she listened and nodded.

"The *Sentry* is currently docking and locking. We should be ready to go in the next few minutes."

Wormy nodded, relaxing into his chair.

[FINISH PREPARATIONS AND TUNNEL AS SOON AS READY. *COMMAND*]

"*Gloro de...* uh... yes, Rega... ah, *Leader*," Hemera caught herself as she stepped forward, habitual expressions jumping from her lips, her hand unconsciously reaching for her forehead. A slight pain seeped into her skull as she wondered what those words meant; why she kept almost saying them.

Hemera motioned to the Bug-Headed Clicker, whom she still didn't know very well. "Cargo Leader, please update me when all craft are secured?"

The Bug-Head seemed to avoid making any social connections, but it clicked as it put in the minimum required work expected of its station.

[**AGREEMENT**]

Hemera enjoyed taking control of the Fangs of the Void, even if it was for simple and routine operations. She paced the second rung as Wormy slowly spun in his seat, two arms behind his wiggly head, the other two folded in front, stalks casually watching the stars. There were several clicks. Hemera looked back at Bug and saw Jeans walking onto the bridge.

[**AFFIRMATIVE**]

Hemera smiled and waved at Jeans, who lifted one of her long, scary-looking arms, extending the sharp digits in a greeting.

"OK! We're ready to go!" Hemera bowed towards Wormy. "On your mark, Leader."

Wormy shook his whole body vigorously, uncrossing his arms disapprovingly.

[NO. YOU FAILED TO OBEY. SOON AS READY, NOT ON MY COMMAND. *CHIDING*]

Hemera's face flushed, her heart beating hard as she realized her mistake. "That's… you're right. You did say that. I'm sorry, Leader. I will do better next time."

Wormy nodded in approval.

[THERE IS HOPE FOR YOU, HEMERA NYX. *AFFEC-TION*]

"Fangs of the Void, let's *snap!*" Hemera shouted, snapping her gloved fingers together.

The old mineral hauler, filled with outcasts, refugees and loners, blurred and stretched into a transparent line that stretched out to both ends of the universe and vanished into the star-speckled dark.

Hemera's boots thunked and clicked as she followed Wormy down the long, densely packed shopping district that covered the transition between the slug-like and humanoid beings, checking over her shoulder to make sure Jeans and Mushroom were following.

While gravity tunnels were simply the connections between two points of mass, only high gravity objects possessed tunnels large enough for spaceships to pass through. As such, some tunnels were much larger and more actively traversed that others. Where those tunnels intersected, there was most likely some kind of refueling depot, space station, or Outpost. Docks, in other words, but for all forms of life from every corner of the galaxy, all sailing through the infinite void of death.

This particular Outpost was the second one Hemera had ever been to. The foundation was a sphere with tall resource-distribution pillars that stood like massive trees with long, sparkling metal branches spreading out into the dark. Those limbs were anchors and refueling stations for smaller spaceships, but they also shone brightly with full-spectrum lights and cold gravity bulbs that radiated down on the worn steel flooring below.

The space between the metal trees was thick with the buzzing of life. Small-scale cargo trolleys criss-crossed on set flight paths. The occasional hotshot pilot weaved between them, and every so often a crash or glancing impact would mark the end of another reckless, fast-paced alien adventurer.

Spacesuits from dozens of large groups moved up and down the Outpost floor, stopping at stalls, stores, and recreational facilities. They used **PLOT** devices to adjust services to their biological needs, make payments, or otherwise transfer and communicate with other aliens, the mysterious handle-twisting technology the only true standard between them. It would have been noisy and smelly if it had an atmosphere, but given the potentially deadly nature of mixing intergalactic lifeforms, everyone remained safely sealed away. The Outpost was open to outer space itself, despite the lights and gravity giving it an illusion of protection from the deadly void.

Some groups were visibly intoxicated; saturating themselves in the instinctively hedonistic relief of life after so much time in the void, they were endlessly ecstatic at the rediscovered existence of life. Hemera had to shove an errant Short-Horned Grunter aside as she, Wormy, Mushroom and Jeans continued down the corridor towards their secretive meeting.

"Leader, you've yet to explain why I'm in the dark about this secretive meeting. It's my job as Sub-Leader to -" A bright light caught her attention, ending her thought as her gloved finger shot upwards. "OH! *WOW!* LOOK AT *THAT!*"

One of Wormy's stalks followed her finger to a spaceship like a snake, each set of scales ringed with independently swiveling engines. It wiggled above the pylons, throwing gentle curves of light as it floated farther into the darkness, the stars absent in the hard lighting of the Outpost.

Wormy watched it float higher for a moment, his other stalks observing Hemera, tracing her outline with fondness and concern, keeping his voice down as he leaned in.

[THE FANGS OF THE VOID ARE IN DANGER, HEMERA NYX. *CONCERN*]

Hemera considered the odd statement, eyes still tracing the wiggling light, frowning. Why was she always in some form of danger? Things seemed to be going well. So well, in fact, that Wormy was bold enough to come to an Outpost in Collected Alliance space . It seemed evidence enough that whatever fears he had were overblown.

It wasn't the first time he'd said something like that, either. Wormy seemed to be possessed of the idea that there were powerful people out to get him, as if anyone could find anyone else in such a vastly open and densely populated universe.

"Really? I don't - *oh!*" Hemera pointed at her elbow, where a tiny stream of vapor was escaping in a thin hiss. She sighed, taking in the reality again.

"I think I need a new spacesuit. I can barely move in this thing, and this is my second leak in the last..." she checked her forearm display. "...*three* days?"

Lifting her arms in evidence of strip after strip of repair tape layered so thickly in the joints it was difficult for her to bend.

"I can't even lift my arms all the way up without almost ripping the frayed bits." She demonstrated. The fabric resisted as the pull against her arms was obvious. A train of beasts encased in armored suits padded past as Wormy leaned back, evaluating her once more.

[I NEVER ASKED YOU. ARE YOU A LARVA/CHILD? *CONCERN*]

Hemera shrugged, still struggling in her suit. "I... guess? I don't think my spacesuit shrunk, so I... I'm *bigger*. I feel bigger." She took a step to the side, flexing her body, feeling it. "*Stronger.* But my helmet still fits, so... I don't know." She shrugged. "Do human heads get bigger?"

Wormy shrugged as well, slowing their advance to a stop as he gestured.

[HOW WOULD I KNOW? *HUMOR* CHECK YOUR PLOT DEVICE. *CONCERN*]

Hemera pulled her **PLOT** out of her chest-socket while Wormy leaned over, giving her basic instructions as she looked up her own biological information, discussing various translation disagreements.

[YOUR PLOT DEVICE DATA STORAGE IS VERY STRANGE. IT DOES NOT FLOW/MOVE LIKE MY OWN. *OBSERVATION*]

The mechanical stomping of Mushroom, who had apparently grown tired of waiting with Jeans, interrupted them. Hemera glared back at it, never sure if she should look at Mushroom through its largest camera eye or at the central fungal bloom in the middle of the glass tank, so she just stared at the whole thing as it waved a robotic hand around in frustration.

[WE DO NOT HAVE TIME FOR LEISURE PURSUITS OR PET DIFFICULTIES. *ANNOYANCE*]

Wormy checked the display on his wiggly arm, then tapped his PLOT reassuringly.

[OUR SUB-LEADER REQUIRES LIFE-SUPPORT ASSIS-TANCE. DO WE LET IT DIE? *QUESTION*]

Mushroom's box leaned back with attitude, only to back off, casting a mean look with a camera-eye in Hemera's direction as it rejoined Jeans.

Jeans, because her suit reminded Hemera of blue denim jeans. The creature inside the spacesuit was oblong, judging by shape. At the top of the suit was helmet, the inside of which was pure darkness. The spacesuit fabric folded in places, giving an even-deeper impression of a big pair of pants - even Jeans' **PLOT**-connection port looked like a pocket. Hidden within the folds, bent arms topped with metal-en-cased clawed gloves lay folded. Hemera had observed those claws cut through a hostile alien's spacesuit once, and was all the more thankful to call Jeans a friend.

The mushroom, on the other hand, was a right bastard. It called again, complex chemical signals transferring into transmitted sound.

[YOUR PET CAN BUY OWN SUIT ON OWN TIME. THIS MEETING –

[THE FANGS USE HEMERA-PLOT FOR PURCHASES. IT HAS NO MONEY OF ITS OWN. THEREFORE, THE FANGS WILL PAY FOR ITS NEEDS. *REFUTE*]

Wormy looked back at the fungus, fully upright, his four wiggly arms crossed hard.

[WE HAVE TIME. *COMMAND*]

Hemera followed the conversation, brow furrowed, her arms crossed, the thin line of air and moisture still gently spraying from her elbow. Mushroom growled as he bowed, and the group started down the wide hallway, cutting across in a different direction.

[*ACKNOWLEDGMENT*]

Hemera followed Wormy, looking up to see ships twinkling between the branched towers, giving her the primal, unconscious impression of being in a forest at twilight. The endless shops, trading posts, bars, and rest-pods sprung up in and among the thick trunks, the detritus scattered, decaying, giving forth new structures that grew and withered in time.

As she looked around at the endless parade of new alien space-suits, she wondered what being in a real forest would be like. Wormy had turned off the main road to follow a tighter, darker space, but even in the side-alley there were spacesuits of variety and design her imagination could never match. The space above them was still thick with alien spacecraft of equal variety and impressiveness. Wormy murmured in the background, the text translation half-read inside her helmet.

[HEMERA NYX. PROMISE TO NEVER LOSE YOUR SENSE OF WONDER. *COMMAND*]

Hemera had been gawking again. She pulled herself together, trying to play it cool as she looked back at Wormy. "Seems like an easy promise to keep. Have you *seen* this place? Or anywhere else? Or any*thing* else?" She couldn't imagine losing that feeling, the shock and delight of experiencing something brand new.

They arrived at a small spacesuit shop in a back-end corner of a more dilapidated roundabout. The shop had a large front window on which a vaguely human-like outline stood. Next to it, another outline that looked like a slug, next to one that looked like a box. The inside of the shop was small, only big enough for one person through the rounded door. Wormy nudged Hemera, then motioned, wrapping one of his thin hands around the handle of his **PLOT** device.

[I WILL GIVE YOU FUNDS SUFFICIENT FOR REASON-
ABLE PROTECTION AND A FEW TOOLS. *STATEMENT*]

He released his hold and extended his hand. Hemera touched the metal pads of his glove to hers, and her wrist display beeped.

[CURRENT: 0]
[INCOMING TRANSFER REQUEST: 2500]

Hemera clicked it through, then stored it on her **PLOT**. She headed for the shop, waving to Jeans and Mushroom, who had taken nonchalant positions nearby.

"Don't worry, I'm sure I'll figure it out how it works," she said, like every other time she encountered something that was so average and common to the rest of the crew that no one seemed to think to offer help, despite the obvious fact that she had no idea what she was doing.

Hemera stepped inside, and the shop door slid shut.

======[A NEW SPACESUIT]======

Some time later, Hemera waddled out in her brand-new space-suit. The skintight fabric was clean, smooth, and patterned with the same electrode-pattern as before. The color, however, was now a shade of light, earthy blue, cut with dashing lines of the familiar white and orange from her old suit's emergency color scheme.

Her external support skeleton, including her rocket boots, had been refurbished. Aside from a few deep pits, they looked almost new. Her helmet, however, remained the same: beaten and dented, the colors faded or chipped to the rusted and naked metal behind. The only thing the shop couldn't replace or refurbish was her life-support pack, endlessly heavy on her back and shoulders in the artificial grav-ity. It wasn't the end of the world; maintaining her life-support pack was one of the first things Hemera had learned to do. Cleaning tubes, brushing filters, and scrubbing converters was second-nature to her now, and the little engines and converters still pumped, wheezed, and gurgled in a steady, reassuring manner.

"It's... uh... *really* stiff." Hemera grunted as she bent her arms, shaking a bit as they came around. Wormy wobbled as he stepped in close, giving Hemera a pat on the back.

[THAT IS HOW YOU KNOW IT IS GOOD FABRIC. *AP-PROVAL*]

"Huurrgghh..." Hemera said, still struggling to bend and flex as Wormy leaned back, barking.

[*HUMOR*]

Hemera stood back up, arms slightly wide, tired of fighting it, suddenly remembering. "Oh, right! You said to get some tools, so I got you a gift. Here!"

She sprung up, throwing her stiff arms around Wormy as she secured a golden ring around one of his helmet tubes, then stepped back as Wormy flicked the ring with a thin hand.

[WHAT IS THIS? *QUESTION*]

"It looks like jewelry, but it's a location tracker," she said, tapping her wrist display, the shifting numbers and arrows moving as she waved her arm around. "Now you'll never get rid of me!"

[DISLIKE BEING TRACKED. *ANNOYANCE*]

Hemera pouted. "...but it's *code-locked*. I'm the only one who can see the signal... uh, according to the instruction screens."

Hemera looked up at Wormy, eyes large and sparkling, a quiver on her lips. He stepped back, then looked away.

[AS IT IS YOU, I WILL ACCEPT. *RESIGNATION*]

Jeans had covered the distance as she ran a circle around Hemera, clicking and chirping, scary arms snapping metal claws together.

[*APPROVAL*]

"Heck yeah! Thanks, Jeans! I knew you'd like the color, huh?" Hemera beamed at her friend as Mushroom approached slowly, nodding his glass case once.

[*APPROVAL*]

"Thanks," Hemera said, nodding back. She looked back at Jeans and Wormy, then nodded. "Thank you, everyone. I can't tell you what a *relief* it is. Look! I can dance!"

Her relief was more true than she thought as she tried to spin and dip in the almost-unyielding fabric, celebrating the absence of all the terror she had been subconsciously holding, the dread of space-suit-failure no longer an active concern.

"OH I ALMOST FORGOT!" she suddenly yelled, causing the aliens to step back in alarm. She slapped open a bulky pouch on her belt, and with dramatic grace, Hemera stepped forward, spinning on the toe of a boot as she pulled and flung a thin synthetic cloak over her.

The metal weave was a deep, mossy green, the edges rimmed with decorative orange symbols and designs. She snuggled into it, securing it around her rubber neck piece.

"*Surprizo!* Now I'm... *incognito.*" She tugged the hood of the cloak over her helmet, trying to appear mysterious under the knee-length fabric. The aliens stared back at her, unsure of what she was doing. She herself wasn't completely sure, but some painfully stuck memory poked at her, pulling an association between adventurers and their cloaks.

Jeans gave her a small, polite applause, and Hemera bowed to the clicking of metal claw-sheathes. Sometimes the aliens seemed so... *human*, but other times they seemed farther away than the farther stars. But there was no need for them to be on board with her at every step. With or without them, she was ready for *adventure*. Hemera took a deep, calm breath, then pointed a stiff arm through the cloak as she motioned down the hallway.

"Don't we have a secretive meeting to get to?"

======[THE SHADOW OF CONSPIRACY]======

The group followed a larger, cluttered street for a time, dodging railed cargo transporters and rowdy gangs before cutting left down a side-passage that opened into a second, smaller road. Threading their way across, they came to the entrance of another alley ringed with trash. Wormy nodded to Hemera as he wrapped an arm around her cloaked shoulder.

[WAIT HERE, AND REPORT TO US IF LAW/POLICE AR-RIVE. *COMMAND*]

"Wha-" Wormy moved close in anticipated of her reaction, and touched his glass to hers. Hemera's entire view was slimy skin pitted with large breathing pores, and four black eyestalks stared back at her.

[SUB-LEADER, YOU ARE SECOND IN COMMAND. FOLLOW THE LEADER. *PLEADING*]

Pleading. Hemera wondered if he'd approve of that contextual in-terpretation. And then she wondered if the reverse happened, that the others sometimes read her emotional state better than she did.

[IF THERE IS TROUBLE, I COMMAND YOU TO LEAVE US AND RETURN TO THE FANGS. YOU WILL IMMEDIATELY TUNNEL OUT OF COLLECTED ALLIANCE SPACE. DO YOU UNDERSTAND YOUR INSTRUCTIONS? *COMMAND*]

Her brow furrowed with sudden concern. She could see it now, the stress and tension in the group. Wormy in particular seemed dis-tracted, cautious. *Worried.*

There was something big going on. Despite the resentment of being left out of the loop, Hemera gave a big thumbs-up with an equally big smile as she pushed past the doubt and annoyance.

"As long as you promise to tell me what's going on at *some* point, then... leave it to me!"

Wormy's little black eyestalks met her eyes, then nodded.

[AGREED. WAIT HERE. *ACCEPTANCE*]

Hemera gave Jeans a fist-bump as Wormy, Mushroom, and her pants-monster friend disappeared into the darkened hallway.

======[ALLEYS AND WAYS]======

Hemera tried to work at the stiffness of her new suit's joints by doing a few squats and jumping jacks, but gave up after a few sweaty minutes of effort. Leaning against the side of the alleyway entrance, she let her eyes wander the hallway, flowing along the shapes of the alien spacesuits that padded, slid, and stamped by.

Absentmindedly, she fiddled with her helmet radio knob. Jeans had left her radio on (most likely because she forgot to turn it off), and after a few clicking twists of a knob, Hemera connected to her helmet. An alien's vocalizations echoed faintly, the sound unrecognized. It was an almost human-sounding garble of syllables and mouth-spits, audible just past the wheezing of Jeans' breathing.

[MAJESTY/MONARCH. I/ENTITY AM/EXIST AS RELIEF/
JOY TO/AS YOUR LIFE-STATUS/ALIVE. *????*]

Hemera crossed her arms and frowned at the translations scrolling inside her helmet. Wormy spoke, the familiar murmuring and bubbling tinny and distant as Jeans sniffled and coughed lightly.

[MAGISTRATE/MINISTER. I DID NOT EXPECT TO SEE
YOU AGAIN. I AM NOT MONARCH/KING. I AM NO ONE.
CAUTION]

There, that almost-human-but-not-quite sound spoke again.

```
[MY LORD/LEADER. FATHER/SOURCE/DIVINITY HAS/
IS UNION THE VOID. YOU/LORD ARE KING/RULER OF
THE KINGDOM/NATION OF/NAMED ??? THE ONE HUNDRED
THOUSAND STAR SYSTEMS ARE YOURS. *STATEMENT*]
```

"...one hundred thousand star systems? What?" Her **PLOT** began
making sense of this new alien's speech, and a slight breeze cooled
her mind as she continued to read the secret conversation. Wormy
was Leader of the Fangs of the Void, sure, but this... the references,
the flowery honorifics and panicked urgencies made no sense to her.
Hemera tapped the glass in front of her face, then checked her wrist
display, smiling slightly at the tracker's numbers before finding it.

```
=======
[TIME: 12047:13:28:01:02]
=======
```

Just a little over six months since Wormy and the Fangs of the
Void rescued her from certain death. Lifetimes, really. Hemera
spread her glove open, inspecting the details she'd insisted on when
upgrading her spacesuit: the hard-covered articulated knuckles with
extra padding, the increased thickness of the metallic-rubber palms,
shiny with small contact points.

Six months ago, she was cowering under some rocks in that gods-
damned hellhole of a planet. Chased by monsters. Shot at by people.
And saved by... someone. And before that... small, sharp shards of
memories. They came randomly cutting their way through her mind
and flesh, each regained memory dreaded as much as desired.

The truth was, she had no idea who Wormy really was or what
kind of life he had before they met. She didn't even know how old he
was, but as the conversation continued to scroll, the outline of a story
began to form. This was bigger than she had thought.

Dark shadows loomed over her as Hemera's eyes grabbed her
attention away from the translating display. Three hunter-robots tow-

ered over her, the Collective Alliance colors on their restrictive suits, the abstract symbol splashed over a shoulder.

"Oh, *shit...*" Hemera breathed. She raised her arms as she stepped forward, trying to be subtle about her thumb finding her transmitter as she then pulled her hood farther down, flashing a wide smile and lowering herself.

"Saluton, *law enforcement hunter-robots.* How can I help you?"

Pulled back into their humanoid form, their thick stiffness was easy to read as 'slow' - but Hemera had once seen one fully unfurled as it chased a fugitive across a plaza. She shivered at the memory as a mechanical snarl replied.

[IDENTIFY THE FOLLOWING ENTITIES]

The closest held up a clawed robotic hand, a small display showing pictures of the Fangs - even herself in her old suit looking stern and focused behind her visor.

Hemera peed a little, then peeked up at the robotic face. "L-looks like a scary group."

The robot leaned in, camera-eyes focusing on her. She swallowed. Her thin green cloak still covered her, but she was sure it was only a matter of time before their processors made the connection.

Why didn't I replace my helmet?

The lead robot leaned in, cameras tracking her, trying to see under her hood.

[IDENTIFY YOURSELF]

"What, me?" Hemera looked around as the other two robots drifted into a half-circle. There was nowhere to go but down the alley after Wormy, or... *up.*

The memory returned of the hapless fugitive smashed and flung by a whirl of sharp steel teeth and thick, jagged claws. She knew she wasn't fast enough, not compared to the mechanical monsters that padded restlessly, watching her, waiting for her to try something.

"I'm... I'm... just an... *outcast.* Just me... just... trying to rest."

The camera-eye bore down on her.

"I'm not breaking any laws," she said convincingly, sure that she was most likely breaking several at that very moment. The robot shifted, scanned her again, then pushed the flat display closer to her visor. The picture switched to Wormy without his helmet, a strange sight in Hemera's eyes, especially since he appeared to be draped in rich fabrics and wearing a silly hat.

[IDENTIFY ENTITY]

"OooOOoohhhh... ah, *no idea?* No. Of course I don't know who that pers- *entity* is. No, that's *crazy.* They... ah... uh..." she stepped back, suddenly aware of the dark ally behind her was flashing and popping. All three robots perked up, expanding metal ears and eyes, exposing long steel teeth as they peered into the commotion.

Hemera grit her teeth as the lights flared again, the unmistakable blasts of weapons echoing up at them. She jumped in front of the robots, waving her arms. "Whoa, hey, look at me, I remember now, they went -" The lead robot shoved her aside as all three plunged headfirst into the alley. She bounced off the wall, landed hard on the steel alley, then scrambled back to her feet as she yelled into her radio.

"GET OUT OF HERE!"

A bright red light flared the moment she entered the darkness after them; the loud, primal hiss of a predatory threat display; the dripping teeth and shiny claws of a hunter-robot moving slowly in her direction. Hemera raised her hands and backed up, exiting the alley. She turned the corner and pressed up against the wall, her hand to her chest.

"That was *scary.*"

She chided herself, trying to calm down. Her friends were in danger. She had to help. There was no other choice - she had to fight. No! She had to follow orders! Wormy's plea came back to her, his command absolutely clear: *Run.*

She tried her radio again. "Jeans, are you-" The noise in her helmet rose to a fevered pitch, gasping and grunting and screaming, the intensity too much. She clicked her radio off.

She needed to think.
No, there was no time. She had to rescue her friends.
No, she needed to get back to the Fangs, to...

A small crowd had gathered at the commotion. Hemera stiffly walked into it, pulling the cloak back over her helmet, standing by, trying to blend into the crowd, biting her tongue, face red with shame, paralyzed by doubt.

"He said to run." Hemera's fists shook as her body fought itself, instinct against command, then clicked her radio back on, a high-pitched gurgling scream filled her helmet. Hemera's body stepped forward, her mind one second behind.

"No. NO! I'M-"

======[TOO LATE]======

At that moment, Wormy emerged from the darkness, hovering two meters in the air, locked in the jaws of a fully unfurled hunter-robot.

Hemera backed up into the crowd again as her eyes met Wormy's stalks. Her fists clenched hard as a second robot emerged from the darkness. It was missing a leg, the empty socket spitting sparks and oil as it scanned the crowd with a lethal intensity, then limped after the first.

"Jeans..."

Hemera looked back at Wormy, who wobbled his head hard, a single murmured bark sounding distant in the crowd as the robot padded down the hallway.

[RUN! *COMMAND*]

Hemera skirted around the second hunter-robot as limped off after the first, then ran, shooting off on her boots down the dark alley-way, flying towards a heap of fabric and blood.

"Oh, Jeans... no..."

Jeans' fabric-like suit had been torn, cut, and ripped apart. Her arms were mangled and broken, sharp claws still clinging to the robotic leg, the corpse of one of the hunter-robots smoldering near-by. Hemera's momentum carried her as she jumped over the robotic scraps and slid on her knees, wrapping her arms around the shredded comrade.

======[CHAIN OF COMMAND]======

The dark helmet had been crushed, shards of dark glass embedded in a horrific mound of flesh. Fluid and semi-transparent flesh flowed out of the suit's holes like wet meat. Hemera stepped back, letting the body gently back down as she saw the naked body of Jeans for the first time; the puke-colored waxy flesh dissolved and turn into goo as it flowed away from the cuts and rips.

Her heart beat hard. Jeans looked nothing like she thought she did: it was horrific to the point of demonic, triggering within her every instinctive revulsion. Her close and trusted friend looked like a monster from the depths of her nightmares. It tore at her, her head suddenly hurting, her chest feeling a hard squeeze. The human mind wasn't built to reconcile affection with the horrific display of decay that spread slowly across the Outpost's dirty alleyway.

A unusual machine stirred as Hemera gripped at her chest, and she jumped back as Mushroom rose slowly, unwrapping robotic arms and legs, revealing the fungus inside the glass once more. It had hardly turned around before Hemera was on it, her shock instantly turning to rage.

"You let Jeans die while you hid in a pile of trash?!"

[I DID NOT SEE YOU. WHAT TRASH PILE DID YOU HIDE IN, HEMERA NYX? *RETORT*]

"I..." Hemera shook. "I... had... *orders*."

[SO DID I. *RETORT*]

A mechanical arm waved at the remains of Jeans.

[WE ALL FOLLOWED ORDERS. THIS IS THE OUTCOME. *STATEMENT*]

"You let Wormy get *captured!*"

[I FOLLOWED THE STRUCTURE OF COMMAND. WHAT DO YOU FOLLOW, HEMERA NYX? *ANGER*]

Jeans continued to flow out of her suit, the flesh actively bubbling and dissolving, organs popping out of pressurized pockets. Mushroom stepped forward, waving a robotic arm.

[JEANS IS DEAD. WORMY IS DEAD. I AM LEADER NOW. WE MUST RETURN TO BASE/HIDEOUT. *STATEMENT*]

Hemera shook her head. Mourning her friend could come later, when she had time to remember the living creature as something - *someone* - other than the pile of rotting demon-meat oozing across the floor in front of her.

Focus on the good I can still do.

"Wormy is *not* dead. They've just taken him." She glanced at her wrist display, then back down the alley, nodding. "We can get him back!"

[WORMY IS A PRISONER/VICTIM OF THE COLLECT-
ED ALLIANCE. *STATEMENT* HE IS DEAD. *LOGIC* A
RESCUE ATTEMPT WOULD ONLY PUT THE FANGS IN DAN-
GER. *ARGUMENT*]

Hemera stomped her foot. "We *can* get him back, but we have to *hurry*-" Mushroom stepped forward, poking her in the chest plate with a thin mechanical hand.

[I AM YOUR LEADER. I COMMAND YOU TO RETURN TO
THE HIDEOUT. *COMMAND*]

Every ability Hemera had to live and thrive among the stars was thanks to Wormy, to his guidance... his *friendship*. She'd be damned if she was just going to lose another friend. And she sure as hell wasn't going to be talked out of it by a gods-damned slime-mold robot. Ignoring the camera-eyes, Hemera leaned in so close she almost touched her helmet to Mushroom's tank, staring right into the fungal fruit that lived in the center.

"You follow the structure of command? You forget your rank, *Energy Distribution Leader*. I am Leader now. The Fangs of the Void are *mine* until Wormy returns." She leaned back out to look once more at the body of Jeans, then back down the hallway out into the main pavilion, the endless crowds continuing along their private business.

The universe was indifferent.

"But... yes. Get back to the *Hideout*. Make sure you're not followed. Get the Fangs docked and locked, but stay there until I return... *with* Wormy." She looked back down the hallway and paused, her hands shaking. "I will not let them take him."

Standing on the ridge between grief and action, Hemera stiffly bent down to Jean's flattened suit, whispering an apology. A quick turn of the handle and she extracted Jeans' **PLOT** from her pocket-socket, then walked evenly to Mushroom.

"We'll have to tunnel the instant we return." Mushroom tucked

Jean's **PLOT** into a side-slot, turning a quizzical camera to Hemera.

[YOU'RE PLANNING ON TRYING TO RESCUE LEADER, DESPITE KNOWING IT IS DEATH TO TRY? *INCREDU-LOUS*]

"I'm not going to rescue *Leader*. I am Leader, and *I* am going to save my *friend*." Hemera had already started back down the hallway, looking at the display on her wrist as she shouted back. "Be ready to go when I get back - that's a *command!*" She turned the corner and sprinted for the elevator, her eyes locked on her tracker numbers that spindled as she ran.

======[RESCUE: HOUR 8]======

Yoink.

The plug came out easily. Hemera held her breath as the robotic pilot jerked erratically for a moment, then slowed to stillness. Stepped forward, she waved a cautious hand in front of the dark robot's camera-eyes. Nothing happened. Relieved, Hemera gave the robot a reassuring pat on its head as she stood upright and stretched.

The inside of the Collected Alliance 'Barouche'-style law enforce-ment spaceship was spacious, with the cockpit open to the rows of locking-seats behind it, which was open to the cargo hold in the back. In the gloom of the mostly powered-off vessel, Hemera felt as if she was hiding in a metallic cave.

She tapped at her forearm display, but Wormy's tracking data re-mained still. They had come through this point before tunneling off to some unknown location, leaving his last known location locked on her display. If there was any way to follow him, it had to start here. She worked her way through her potential crimes as she approached the barouche's control console: trespassing in a Collected Alliance repair depot, tampering with security measures, deactivating a service ro-bot. And now, hopefully, data theft. It didn't matter - she was going to find Wormy, get back to the Fangs, and never enter CA space again. All she needed was a direction.

Her heart beat hard as she tapped the forward console's buttons thoughtfully with a gloved finger. The displays were lit up with all sorts of runes and glyphs, the default language of the CA unreadable to her. Worse, the console was rejecting her inputs, the biometric data from the contact points on her gloves unrecognized by the half-broken spaceship. She frowned as she crossed her arms and considered the encoded console in front of her, then glanced back at the dark, unresponsive robot.

"Where did they take him?"

The robot did not move. Hemera sighed, then ran her hand over the console and wrapped her fingers around the "dummy" **PLOT** device, then twisted and extracted it as the console went dark.

Robots couldn't use real **PLOT**s. The strange technology, a mystery to even the most advanced aliens, required some amount of biological material to activate, binding to the user. Dummy-**PLOT**s weren't mysterious like real **PLOT**s were, as they were basic permission-keys that allowed automated pilots to use spaceships. Extracting her **PLOT** from her chestpiece, Hemera took a big breath that echoed in the small space between her face and glass, then looked back at the robot once more.

"This is a terrible idea." She shoved in her **PLOT** and twisted the handle. The console immediately lit up as she took a step back. The displays flickered and snapped as the symbols twisted and wiggled into forms she could recognize. A flash from the front windshield caused her to duck, the bright flare of a nearby spaceship speeding by spiking her adrenals. The light passed as quickly as it came.

"Not looking for me... I'm not here..." Hemera whispered to herself as she pulled her **PLOT** out and pushed the dummy back in. The consoles went dark and then lit up again - and this time, the displays stayed readable.

"Yus!" Hemera did a fist pump, glad for the first success since she started chasing after Wormy. Displays usually kept the settings from the last connected **PLOT** - a lesson she'd learned the hard way when

she accidentally overrode the *Striker* while doing repairs on the central processor. All three hundred of the crew and eight hundred passengers were more than a little upset with her that day. Still, having her **PLOT** connected to a CA ship - even briefly to a broken one - was a horrible idea, as evidenced by what was already flashing brightly on a side-console.

```
=======
[!UNREGISTERED USER!]
[!BROADCASTING SECURITY WHISTLE!]
=======
```

Pushing the robot aside and bending under the console, Hemera found the bundle of wires connecting the display to the transmitter and gave a hard yank. The flashing vanished as the display went dark.

"C'mon Hemera, go faster. Find it... find it..." she whispered to herself as she pulled the travel list from the navigation console. Wormy's tracker had logged this location right before they tunneled. He was a prisoner. They'd take him to a prison ship, or some sort of transport. A known location, and somewhere nearby to increase tunnel egress accuracy. She continued to scroll, holding her forearm display, looking for matching numbers. The last logged location was locked to the time, so all she had to do was find a tunnel event that matched the time with a known destination.

"Found you!" She glanced back and forth a few times, just to be sure. The times matched, and the location was a prisoner transport ship only a light year away. Hemera sighed as she downloaded the coordinates onto her glove and transferred them to her **PLOT**.

"Thanks for the help, friend, I..." Hemera paused as she tapped the top of the quiet robot thoughtfully. The camera-eyes stared back blankly, but Hemera found herself lost in them as she whispered to herself. "... am I the dumbest person ever? *What* was the plan, Hemera? Just fly the *Sparrow* directly at a prisoner transport spaceship? They'll let me land, right? Just walk in, grab a prisoner, and take off? *No problem."*

"Hrrmmmghhh..." she said as she sat down to ponder, giving the

robot a spiteful little push. The spike of joy she felt at finding Wormy's location had soured at the prospect of finding a way through dense Alliance security. Was Mushroom right? Was this some idiotic tantrum, an easy way to get blasted into bits or grabbed by the CA and enslaved for the rest of her life? The robot continued to lean to the side, only to suddenly fall off the pilot seat and crash noisily to the steel floor. Hemera started at the sound, then glanced up at the gravity bulbs glowing dully on the ceiling. She watched the bulbs for a moment, then looked back at the console. The dummy was still firmly inserted, the still-working displays operational. She looked back at the robot sprawled across the floor, then back at the empty pilot chair.

"OH!"

======[RESCUE: HOUR 29]======

The plan was working.

Or it had been. Sweat stabbed at the edges of her heavy eyelids. Grunting, she gave another tug on the bulky yellow lockbox covering the emergency airlock handle. The lockbox was, in Hemera's exhausted opinion, too large for simply securing a maintenance airlock. The angry molten line she had been working on would take her at least an hour to finish, and there seemed to be another set of hardened rods past the ones she was still trying to slice.

"I won't let them." The phrase endlessly reverberated in Hemera's skull, her eyes blurry, her body heavy and slow. Shaking her head hard, she holstered her laser cutter. The brightness of the small red dwarf dominating the area hid the rest of the stars, turning the void pitch black. The long, curved transport-ship was safe enough, hidden as she was in a shadow on the hull. The stolen barouche covered her like camouflage, as both spaceship hulls made of the same material. Between that and the darkness of the shadow, Hemera was, for the moment, hidden.

Peeking out from under the barouche, Hemera tracked a few bright dots flying at a distance, following the flow of the hull. She had managed to convince the transport ship's auto-nav that she was the robot by using its metal fingers on the console. The computer spat directions to the repair bay. But that was ten hours ago, and someone would have noticed a missing spaceship by now. Maybe sending notifications, chains of command...

The clock was ticking.

Slapping the **RAMA** to her holster, Hemera stood fully upright, trying to crack her spine as she leaned back, feeling the weight of her lack of sleep like a sparkling burden. It only took a few magnetic-locking steps to get back to the *Sparrow*. The underside faced her, one towing-claw gripping the barouche, the other locked firmly to the prison carrier. Hemera gave a final tug at the towing claw connected to the transport, making sure it was secure before she stomped a magnetic boot to the *Sparrow's* underside.

Pausing, Hemera studied her spaceship from underneath. The stubby wings, charred at the edges. The paint, faded and chipped. The small dimples of micro-impacts. The rectangular handle, ringed by safety stripes. The handle...

A smile grew on Hemera's tired face. The *Sparrow* wobbled between its two anchor points as Hemera planted both boots securely over the handle and grunted. Another hard pull and she unlocked the *Sparrow's* industrial beam-cutter, hefting it in the zero gravity, wrangling with the thick, curled cord that came spilling after it.

The chance to use the powerful cutter had been rare, and her lack of experience made handling it a struggle. It was more than enough to cut the lock, but she remembered the danger: firing for more than thirty seconds would risk melting the barrel. If the barrel melted, the beam would find a new way out - most likely in every direction, possibly all at once. Hemera breathed heavily as she tried to level the bulky tool at the big yellow lockbox, the *Sparrow* wobbling between its two anchor points, her eyes tired, her muscles sore and dull.

Click.

It cut clean through the lock. And kept going, slicing a long, red line out of the shadows as she was shoved backwards from the force, a molten flare smoking across the prisoner-transport's hull. Regaining her balance, she whispered a long streak of swear words, hoping nobody noticed that their prison spaceship had gained a angry red line along the surface. The line quickly faded as she shrugged, letting the *Sparrow* retract the cutter as she jumped back to the airlock. Some jagged chunks still stuck to the hull, glowing red in the dark, while most of the lock-box gently lifted away. Shoving aside the floating chunks of half-molten steel, her nearly numb fingers wrapped around the emergency handle and twisted.

It only took one try to see it too tightly screwed in to budge by hand. Wasting no time, she pulled her **RAMA** and flicked the extension rod. Shoving the heavy hooked end under the handle and anchoring her boots against the hull, she shoved. Slowly, then all the once, the handle gave way.

The pressure from behind the airlock screamed out of the opening crack, flinging Hemera back as her boots kept their grip on the hull. Her back hit the hull first, slamming her life support pack into the thick metal skin of the ship. The pack held, but the impact flung her forward, sending her face-first back at the opening and slamming her chest into a jagged edge of semi-molten metal.

Her gloved hands grasped at her upper left chest as she yelled and sobbed. Moisture and air sprayed from the open cut as her helmet filled with loud pinging. Large warnings in alarm-red filled the edges of her vision as she pulled her fingers back. It was only a small trickle of blood as the wound and the suit seared as much as cut, but small sprays continued to rip painfully into the void. Hemera had already reached for the roll of repair tape and ripped off a generous portion.

Slap. The thin streams of moist air slowed to a stop as she kept pressure on it; her face twisted as the adhesive chemicals soaked into her burnt skin exposed from the melted fabric. The pinging in her helmet stopped as the body of her suit re-pressurized.

Breathing heavily, she looked around for her **RAMA**. It was gone, floating somewhere out of sight. Raising her arm, she held out her hand, clicking it completely wide for a moment, then letting her fingers relax. She remembered the time she broke her hand from pulling the **RAMA** in zero gravity. It was a painful lesson on velocity that she only needed to learn once.

A few more clicks and the **RAMA** drifted into view, coming right for her. Grabbing the elongated stick, she retracted the pry-bar and dialed down the cutter to the lowest setting in an easy, habitual motion. She smiled through the pain as she touched the tip of the beam-emitter to the fresh patch of tape.

"Space adventures sure are rough."

She raked the small, bright light gently over the tape. The heat saturated her flesh as it melted and fused to the torn fabric and her burnt skin. A burn on top of a burn, fused to the tape, fused to the fabric. She would have to cut those bits of skin off the next time she wanted to leave her spacesuit. She thundered with pain. Checking once more to make sure the seal was complete, she shoved the **RAMA** back into the holster and leaned over, her hand gently covering her new wound, her eyes squeezed tight, feeling the pain wash over her, tears forming in the edges of her dark vision.

"...ow." Standing over the now-open emergency airlock, she lifted her hand as she opened her squeezed eyes, looking over the fresh wound once more. The repair tape was a garish, ugly slap across the lovely blue. Liquid fire flooded her blood. Why was she being so careless, so stupid, so gods-damned *slow?*

Wasn't this life or death?

Wasn't this *adventure?*

Her rage, her pain, and her frustration all mixed into a biological fire she felt consuming her, every ounce of her body dry and ready fuel. She took a completely deep breath as she leaned back and howled her vengeance to the absent gods in the silent void.

"THIS WAS A BRAND-NEW SPACESUIT!"

====== **[UN/EXPECTED]** ======

Hemera's sweaty brow peeked around the corner, her gentle panting causing bursts of fog on the inside of her helmet's glass visor. She could hear the thudding of robotic feet echoing down the well-lit hallway as she ducked back into the shadows. The tracking number was steadily decreasing, almost back to zero.

Wormy. It had to be him. Her heart beat faster, excitement flooding her body. As if on cue, the lead guard stepped into view. Something like a long-limbed gorilla in a formal military uniform strode confidently forward. Hemera wondered why so many species insisted on putting things on their heads, as this one had a large, fancy hat in the Collected Alliance colors, complete with puffy curls of hair flowing down on the sides.

Is that his hair? Hemera wondered as she ducked back farther. A much smaller green robot in a white coat squeaked and chirped after the larger gorilla. Following them was a robotic guard that tugged on a chain.

Hemera held her breath - *Wor... no!*

The next creature ambled into view, following the pull of the chain. It almost looked human - four limbs, white spacesuit with a bright yellow symbol on it, even an almost-human face contained in the rounded helmet - but alien's head had some dark circular appendage that flared into black spikes in the back. Hemera shook her head. No human hair could retain that kind of shape.

Definitely not human.

The chain continued to pull as they made their way down the hallway, and Wormy finally came into view, his bronze spacesuit scuffed and dirty. Both chained creatures walked with a slow slump, and Hemera grit her teeth as her eyes flashed in the dark. The final robotic guard stomped behind them. Hemera stayed perfectly still, then slid noiselessly into the hallway after them. Her fingers naturally twisted the knobs on her **RAMA** as she quietly stepped up behind the rear robotic guard.

A clean puncture through the center of the processor. Hemera grabbed the robot as it fell, trying to soften the fall, but it slipped out of her grasp. The prisoner line stopped at the clattering racket, but Hemera didn't wait for them to turn around. Blasting her rocket boots, she flipped high over the prisoners and landed hard between the gorilla and the front guard. She spun, delivering a hard kick to the gorilla's gut as she turned to place the energy beam through the robot's processor.

The small green robot screamed and fumbled trying to extract a weapon from its coat. Hemera launched herself forward and grabbed its leg, spun hard, and threw the robot as hard as she could right as the gorilla was standing up. The impact sent both sliding down the hallway.

"*RUN-*" Hemera turned to the human-like alien, only to find it was already sprinting down the hallway in a panic, the loud clanging of metal-clad shoes echoing as it slid into a turn and vanished down another corridor. Hemera watched it go, then strode over to her friend, who looked up at her from where he'd been shoved.

[HEMERA NYX. *SHOCK*]

Hemera smirked at the shocked eyestalks. "I'd ask if you want to be rescued, but at this point I really don't give a shit. *Let's go.*" His murmurs sounded tired as she helped him to his feet. Face sweaty, eyes narrow with pain and anger, it only took two quick, clean cuts before Wormy's bindings fell off. He stumbling to his rubbery knees as Hemera grabbed under an arm. She glanced back at the commanding gorilla-type, who was standing back up, long arms waving as it shouted commands to the small green robot.

Wormy seemed to be recovering, his stalks moving more steadily as he stood upright, radiating some more of his commanding presence.

[WE HAVE NO CHANCE OF ESCAPE. *STATEMENT*]

"*HA!*" The snorting laugh came out involuntarily, and Hemera felt a sudden onset of giggles as she started pulling him towards the way she'd come. "You're probably right, Wormy. I know I shouldn't have come. It was a dumb idea, but you know what? *I rescued you anyway.*"

Wormy followed, trying to run on his bendy legs, clearly worked over and injured as they crammed into the maintenance airlock. The doors began sliding shut as the lights in the hallway shifted and flashed as deafening alarms, and Hemera's giggles quickly fell into a stern conviction.

"We gotta go!"

====== [ESCAPE] ======

Hemera's boot pressed against Wormy as she shoved him into the *Sparrow's* cockpit, his four arms waving in discomfort.

"You... don't... *hhrr...* have bones... so... get *in* there!"

Hemera got Wormy all the way in with a hard shove then shoved herself in after him, squeezing under his squishy body as she slammed her **PLOT** into the console. Wormy's stalks were transfixed on the barouche the *Sparrow* was still gripping. Disconnecting the claw from the large transport spaceship, Hemera gently tapped the *Sparrow's* side-boosters, pushing quickly away as the CA spaceship drifted in the opposite direction.

[WHERE DID YOU GET A COLLECTED ALLIANCE BA-
ROUCHE? *CONFUSION*]

Hemera grunted. "I'll tell you later - right now we need to *get.*" Within a few moments, they could see the length of the ship, emergency lights lighting up across the hull like spreading wildfire, a dramatic contrast of light and dark. The prison ship continued to shrink into the distance as a squad of fighters arrived, scanning the hull with bright lights, tracing the outline of her cut across the side.

[THERE IS NO POSSIBLE WAY THIS WILL WORK. *CER-
TAINTY*]

"That's what they said about me rescuing you." Hemera didn't look back as she tapped at the navigation panel, then shoved Wormy to the other side to work the switches.

[HEMERA NYX, NOW IS THE TIME TO GO! *ALARM*]

"Yeah, I know! I just put in the tunnel for... *oh*." She looked up from the console to see an entire platoon of fighters headed directly for them, then snapped her fingers. She had opened her mouth to yell a challenge, but to her surprise, the lead fighter burst into an orange cloud of flame and smoke as the other fighters peeled away, scrambling into an unexpected fight. Hemera's wide eyes only caught a flash of the yellow spaceship with the bulbous rear engine as it sped by. The strange human-like alien with the odd head-appendage saluted Hemera, winked, and disappeared into the dark.

Hemera's cheeks suddenly felt warm as she looked away for a moment, then back up as the fighters regained their formation, but it was too late. She slammed the tunneling button as a taunt escaped her lips.

"You've been Nyxed!"

The *Sparrow* stretched and then vanished into deep space, a volley of lasers and plasma bolts filling the empty space.

====== [ANSWERS AND QUESTIONS] ======

Nowhere in the universe was as safe as a random void location, so the instant they arrived in the empty nothing Hemera found her fingers working on the latches of her helmet. There was a puff as the front swung wide, and Hemera gasped deeply, as if she had been holding her breath the entire time. Her heavy breathing calmed as she relaxed, feeling the sweat evaporate on her face.

"Did I really just say 'you've been Nyxed'? What..." Hemera started chuckling to herself as the soft body behind her mumbled and shifted, clearly uncomfortable in the tight space.

[WHY DID YOU RESCUE ME? *QUESTION*]

Hemera sighed. After a few moments to collect herself, she twisted, looking back at the stalks through his clear visor, her own visor swinging on worn hinges.

"Did you really expect me to just run away? To just abandon you like that?"

[I EXPECTED YOU TO FOLLOW ORDERS. *STATEMENT*]

Hemera grunted. "See, I *did*. I..." Hemera's mood dropped as she remembered Jeans bleeding out into a dirty back alley. And that smug mushroom in a clear tank pushing back.

"When you got captured, I became Leader, so... I decided that rescuing you was a direct command from the Leader of the Fangs of the Void - me."

There was silence as Wormy considered it.

"Wormy..." Hemera paused. The question had been on her mind for a while. In fact, it had been on her mind from the moment she first woke up in that rest-pod, the strange pile of bronze spacesuit still and asleep in the corner. "Why did you rescue me, way back then?"

It seemed like a big question for Wormy to ponder, but he responded almost instantly, the answer apparently easy.

[THERE IS NO WHY. THERE WAS NO CHOICE TO MAKE. *STATEMENT*]

"Hm." Hemera smiled as she turned back to the controls. They sailed through the random location in silence for a time before she spoke again.

"So... who are you, really? You're the Leader of the Fangs, but that's not they took you, right? It's something else?"

Wormy shrugged, all four arms moving up and down as best he

could, given they were shoved close together.

[I WISH THAT I WAS ONLY THE LEADER OF THE FANGS
OF THE VOID. *REGRET*]

"Can't you… like, *renounce* whatever it is they're chasing you for?
Would they leave you alone, then?"

[I CANNOT CHANGE WHO OTHERS THINK I AM. *SAD-
NESS*]

Hemera frowned hard as she turned to check the console. "Well,
we got away clean. We're in a random location two light years away,
and your little tracker doesn't work at tunneling distance."

Wormy considered for a moment.

[WHERE ARE YOU TAKING ME? *QUESTION*]

Hemera frowned at the dumb question. "Back to the *Hideout*,
dummy. Where else?" Wormy seemed to relax at the reply, but Hemera couldn't shake the feeling that something about him had changed.
Tossing his head, he reached out a delicate arm in an overly dramatic
fashion, rubbing at the cockpit glass thoughtfully.

[THE HIDEOUT. THE FANGS OF THE VOID. A CHILD'S
DREAM. *DISMISSAL* THE TRUTH IS THAT I AM -]

"The *fuck* did you just say?" Hemera exploded, twisting around to
look the worm right in the stalks. "The *Hideout* is a… *child's dream?* That
truth is, *what*, life sucks sometimes, and you're all *sad* about it?"

Wormy looked back at her, his stalks shock-still as she poked a
gloved finger in the middle of his visor.

"*GROW UP!* You think you're the only royal exile wandering the
stars? We're like a dime a dozen out here!" She waved her hand vigorously before turning around to focus on flying, her rant nowhere near
finished, her front visor swinging wildly as she gestured.

"The entire galaxy was against you, and you fought *back*. You made your own home, your own *nation*, just by you being *yourself!* No choice to be made? I owe everything to you, and the Fangs! You're my h... my *friend*, Wormy. I mean that."

```
[THANK-
```

She turned around again. "But by sweet merciful Leoborah's big soft tiddies if you talk shit about the *Hideout* again I *will* eject you from this cockpit. Understood?"

Wormy nodded, stalks retracted.

```
[UNDERSTOOD, LEADER. *RESPECT*]
```

Hemera nodded, then smiled to herself as she turned back to the controls.

```
======[RISK]======
```

Their next tunnel was remarkably accurate, considering the unusual weight distribution in the cockpit. She cleared her throat again as they sailed towards the Outpost.

"I'm thirsty, and hungry. I bet you are, too. If we're going to make it back to the *Hideout,* we're going to need supplies. Fuel, tunnel cans, water, food."

Wormy murmured an agreement.

```
[RESUPPLY AT THIS OUTPOST IS UNAVOIDABLE.
*STATEMENT*]
```

She wiggled under the worm-man to check the navigation console, making sure the threshold value was decreasing, feeling a strong sense of camaraderie with Wormy even as she had to lift him up to read.

```
======
[LAMP CONNECTION]
[SIGNAL: 889]
======
[THRESHOLD: 00:06]
======
```


Hemera smiled as she turned back to her flying.

"We're almost at the second Lamp. We're right on track... I have to set the ship to auto-curve at the apex, I can't do it manually with you in here," she grumbled as she wriggled back to the front console, now fully talking to herself.

"I'm going to set it for... half-distance past the first. That should keep us... far enough from the Outpost to avoid attention," she said, typing in some instructions from a spotty memory.

"OK... yes... I think that's it," she said, pulling her hesitant hand back. She squinted at the buttons for a few moments more, then shook her head as she waved dismissively. "Yeah, it's fine, it's fine."

It would still take a few hours to get there. It was quiet in the cockpit. So quiet, in fact, that she could hear Wormy's breathing through his spacesuit; his wet, rattling intake kept rhythmically giving way to what could only be described as a 'fart noise.'

Rattle. *Fart.* Rattle. *Fart.* A louder rattle. A long, wet, juicy *fart.*

Hemera couldn't hold it in. Wormy shifted as she howled with laugher. He looked her over, then tilted his head as well, his body convulsing, deep barking sounds mixing with her snorts and wheezing.

[*HUMOR*]

Hemera let the laughter swell and ebb for some time. She didn't know what Wormy had been laughing about, but she figured it didn't matter. She just rescued a prisoner from the Collected Alliance right out from under their noses, still nearly blasted to bits, but whole and sane all the same.

She sighed again, this time in a warm feeling of contentment, letting her eyes close for a moment.

======= [REWARD] =======

Hemera woke instantly at the chime and elbowed Wormy as she cleared her dry throat.

"Hey, wake up."

Wormy rumbled and farted, slowly rolling around to consciousness as Hemera silenced the navigation computer's alarm. The *Sparrow* had automatically reduced the primary engine, bringing them to a clean, silent standstill a hundred thousand kilometers from the distant Outpost. The view outside hadn't changed - the endlessly thick sparkle of distant lights bore down upon the tiny spaceship. Hemera pondered as she began buttoning up her spacesuit.

"This is a different Outpost than the one we got ambushed in, but we're still in CA space. Do you..." she paused, considering. This was all new to her. She was making decisions on long-forgotten adventure novels and movies, dramatic stances and defiant statements habitually bubbling just under the surface of her foggy brain.

"Do you... have any friends on this Outpost? Someone from your past? Someone who could help us?"

[A FRIEND OF MINE IS AN ENEMY OF THE COLLECTED ALLIANCE. I WOULD NOT GIVE SUCH RISK TO A FRIEND. *SADNESS*]

"Oh."

[I SHOULD REMAIN HIDDEN. *STATEMENT*]

"Yeah, obviously." Hemera began shuffling for her missing spacesuit pieces. "You get to take a zero-gravity nap while I do all the risky work."

The wobbly alien looked at Hemera as she struggled to the hatch, giving her a pat on the back.

[AS EXPECTED, LEADER. *PRIDE*]

"*Humf,*" Hemera said, a smile tugging at the edges of her mouth as she pulled the release handle. The cabin flooded with bubbly rainbows that vanished so quickly she wasn't even sure she saw it, the hatch hissing into the silent nothing.

Floating, they both floated out into the empty of outer space, glad for the extra floating room as they bent and stretched, working the kinks out of their respective floating bodies as they went over the plan, floating, listing what to buy and where to get it as they floated.

"Let's go over the plan once more. You're going to stay here until I come back. You still have your tracker -" Hemera motioned to the golden ring Wormy mindlessly fiddled with, "- so we can go radio-silent unless there's an emergency."

[HERE ARE THE FUNDS. SPEND AS MUCH AS NEEDED. RETAIN THE REST FOR YOURSELF. *STATEMENT*]

Wormy reached out a thin hand to connect with Hemera's glove.

[CURRENT: 83]
[INCOMING TRANSFER REQUEST: 65410641]

"That's..." Hemera paused. She'd never had this much to herself before. It was a *lot.*

[IT SHOULD BE MORE THAN ENOUGH. *STATEMENT*]

Hemera took a breath, trying to bypass the mix of emotions swelling up inside as she accepted, then turned to face Wormy, the stars dancing off his glass as they softly spun around each other. He curled one of his thin hands into a ball, a small digit poking up from the middle. Hemera smiled and returned the imitation of a thumbs-up, then turned back to her spaceship.

[HEMERA NYX. *ATTENTION*]

Hemera spun in space to see all four of Wormy's arms out-stretched as they gently folded around her. It took a second before Hemera realized it was one of the best hugs she'd ever received, and she gave him an affectionate squeeze in return.

"Are you going to be OK out here by yourself? Your **PLOT** is charged, right? I should be back way before you run dry." She paused, pulling back from his boneless embrace. "And no void-walking, right?"

[I WILL REMAIN AND CONTINUE TO LIVE. I WILL SEE THE END OF MY STORY WITH MY OWN EYE-STALKS. *PRIDE*]

"And that will be a long time from now." Hemera entered the *Sparrow* and closed the hatch, the cockpit bursting with bubbles for a moment. Wormy tapped on the glass, talking through their radios.

[YOU'VE NEVER BEEN ON AN OUTPOST ALONE. WILL YOU BE SAFE? *CONCERN*]

"Leave it to me!" Hemera smiled as she blasted a thumbs-up in his direction, the warmth and pressure of his hug still around her body.

He drifted back as the *Sparrow's* primary engine flared to life.

=======[//3//]=======

It was the third Outpost Hemera had ever been in. She shifted her metal-cloth bag on her shoulder as she walked, trying not to look up so much, but it was difficult. Instead of the twisting metal trees of the last Outpost, this one was *geometric*. Long, tapered pyramids rose high from the central octahedron base. The shapes branched out, bent, and branched again as they adjusted to accommodate spaceships of all shapes and sizes.

Math. That's what the shapes reminded her of. Rubbing the flat of her visor with her palm, she tried to rub the dull stabbing out of her eye socket, then gave up with a frustrated grunt as she walked down a steel street, cautiously weaving between the clumps of oddly shaped spacesuits going about their strange business.

Despite the different scenery above, the floor of the Outpost was more or less the same as the others she'd been to: a network of brightly lit roads on the surface hiding the twisting alleys and passages that tangled together just under, layers of shadows and beams of light that criss-crossed down, down, and down. An enormous neon sign radiated pink and purple as she walked by. The glyphs and symbols that flashed and popped gave an almost party-like atmosphere to the crowd of Short-Horned Grunters that milled around the entrance.

Hemera wondered what service that business provided as she turned, following a small path down into the shade of an overpassing express lane. Walking down some darkened stairs, she eyed two small groups of Thin-Spikers sitting, chirping softly to themselves as she passed quietly by. They seemed to pay her no mind, but there was no way of really knowing. For all she know, they could be alerting someone farther up that another loner ripe for harvest was headed their way.

It *was* scary. She felt a shiver up her back as she left the groups on the stairs behind and headed toward a wider, more public road. Safety in numbers was undeniably true. It was unusual to see anyone in a group of fewer than ten or twenty. The Fangs had reason to try to avoid bringing attention to themselves, but they ran that risk with too small of a group as well.

Loners - those banished from even fellow outcasts - were the most despised class of aliens in the galaxy, and the most feared. Who knows what evils a loner had inflicted to be cast adrift in the endless nothing? A group of Tall-Necked Nodders gave her wide berth as she walked out of the darkness into the well-lit road. They ambled past, fearful of making eye contact with her visor, which she had dialed down to be near black.

Still, there was a newness to the outing. Her eyes traced a cluster of game-machines as she passed by, covered in all manner of knobs and buttons, making shapes and colors change, adding up scores, spitting out tinny electric music. There were always a few aliens around game-machines, smacking the controls with paws, tentacles, and other types of hands, their space-suited appendages tapping furiously while others gathered around for the free entertainment.

Her rubberized magnetic boots paused as she looked up at a large metal sign. She had traveled to the edge of what she would classify as the 'humanoid' section, the glowing arrows pointing in different directions along with an outline of different body-shapes. She traced an arrow with a gloved finger, then turned, following a nervous group of creatures whose spacesuits covered in small rollers, allowing them to slide along the steel ground.

Hemera tried to not stare at the other, larger groups of aliens as they walked, waddled, slid, and rolled through the area. They minded their own business so long as others minded theirs, but she couldn't help but sneak peeks at the endless parade, making up names as they flowed by.

The Man-sized Three-Arms, their extra limbs holding on to each other as they floated above her.

Two-Headed Clappers, endlessly clapping with their weird split-helmets, trying to cross the street in front of the Water-Filled Runners, the sight of which reminded Hemera of someone in her forgotten past as they jiggled and wobbled out of the way.

The Big Stompers, clearly out of their preferred zone, too large for the side-roads in this area, walking slowly, giving other groups time to get out of the way.

She stepped aside to give whatever the hell those… *things* were a wide, safe distance, only to suppress a smile as a gang of waist-high Jumping Egg-Runners sprinted around her, oblivious to her loner-status as they hopped and squeaked by.

More aliens continued on their own business as she moved farther into the blob-like section, following boxed slugs onto a moving pathway as the road took on a more gentle curve, the architecture becoming more accommodating to those who moved closer to the ground. Finally, she found what she was looking for. Tucked farther back in the shadow of a small warehouse, the large glowing tank was unmistakably exactly like Wormy had described: filled with what could only loosely be described as 'living things' that swam mindlessly in murky, greenish water.

Hemera waved down the alien behind the small glass storefront. Rousing itself from what appeared to be a nap, the grumbling worm-like person ambled over and pressed its face into the window. It looked very much like what Hemera imagined Wormy looked like without his suit on, minus an eye stalk and a limb.

She pointed to the tank, put a finger in the air, and then curved her arm in the way Wormy had shown her. The alien behind the glass observed her for a moment, remaining stalks tracing her outline, then pulled a lever. The bottom of the tank opened as an open glass cylinder entered the and filled with water. At the bottom of the tube, a small purple orb began melting, the color dissolving into the tube. Hemera peered in as a wobbly blur shot forward, grabbed the orb, and wrapped itself around it. The clerk pulled the lever and the cylinder retracted. There was a mechanical 'thunk' sound as the container re-emerged and rolled down a track.

The clerk scooped it up with a naked tentacle arm for her to see through the glass. It was a clear glass cylinder capped with a cheap metal top. Inside, somewhat blurry from goo, was a bulbous, sinewy creature that shook and burped. It wiggled its blue little eye-stalks vacantly in the water, sucking on the purple orb as it looked back at her. Hemera watched the barely living blob for a while, then shrugged. A small display lit up, and she touched a metal pad next to it, shifting the characters into something she could read.

[??? COST: 223]

A button on her glove logged the request, then she touched the handle to her **PLOT**, which extracted the money. A delightful chime rang out as she touched the panel again. The alien nodded as it dropped the little pod into an airlock shelf, which showered it with rainbow bubbles, then popped the container out on the other side of the glass wall.

She picked it up. Two dumb eyestalks stared back at her as the creature sucked on the diminishing orb. Wormy didn't tell her what he needed the creature for, only mentioning that he would 'greatly appreciate' it. She pondered for a moment, still looking at the blob as it sucked the remaining bits of purple orb into itself. She rubbed gently at her recent wound as she pondered. It had to be a life-form that produced... what? A rare drug? Or was it a new pet? Or... just a... nice treat? After Wormy's abduction and torture, Hemera figured he could use any one of those.

She gave it a little shake. It wibbled and wobbled in the fluid. They stared at each other for a few moments more, then Hemera placed it into her bag, already heading back the way she came.

She still had plenty of money left, even after buying the fuel containers, tunneling canisters, nutrient-sacks, and water tubes that filled her bag, so she paused at a small kiosk in the middle of a hallway. It was an automated machine that held tiny figures, sculptures, and space-safe stickers. Her eyes hungrily searched the small knick-knacks on display. A little memento of that time she rescued her friend Wormy from the Collected Alliance and possibly saved a galactic civilization in the process. Perhaps a sticker, or...

"*Ow!*" Her hand grasped her chest as her recent wound flared painfully, then jumped, spooked, as her eye caught something moving in the reflection of the kiosk's glass front. No, not something... it was...

Her. She was bent over, looking at the exposed bones and raw flesh of her hand with empty sockets. *She...*

"*Ah*, nope. *Nope!*" Hemera shook her head. Blinking hard, trying to pull herself back together, she focused on the pain on her chest for a moment, then forced herself to look again. The reflection was simply one of a human-like creature, sitting by itself, staring vacantly at a red patch in their five-fingered hand.

A *very* human-like human-creature.

It took a full minute for her to turn around, eyes wide, jaw slacked. The creature was bent over, drink-tube attached to their helmet, the color and cut of their suit unfamiliar but somehow overwhelmingly intimate. The creature inside the suit... it... they...

Her body walked itself slowly forward, fighting through the shock, too alarmed to speak.

His helmet turned to hers.

======[A HUMAN BEING IN SPACE]======

Both helmets faced each other across the walkway.

Hemera was operating on instinct, standing stock-still, breath-held in shock, then vigorously shook her head and strode over to him. She covered the distance quickly, but found her mouth was useless. Her hand shot out instead, her whole body buzzing. The stranger regarded her with an equal amount of shock and caution, looking back and forth between her hand and her ruddy, intense face before speaking in an unfamiliar language.

[I AM NOT LOOKING TO BE AROUND PEOPLE. *CONCERN*]

Hemera swallowed, then squeaked. *"Ah... what... did... you..."*

The suited figure tilted his helmet, this time speaking the language she understood: "Oh, you... are... are there more of your people around?"

He looked around as he shoved the piece of fabric into a pouch, then focused his attention back on her, standing up suddenly and digging into her unguarded eyes. He was a full head above her, towering like a mountain of longing and impossibility that spoke the language of humans.

His concern was plain and obvious. "Who are you? What home-ship?" Hemera stared back, mouth open, brain empty. The man cocked an eyebrow and waved his hand in front of her. "Uh… *saluton?*"

Hemera swallowed again, forcing her mind to push past the shock, to get some words out. *"I'm sorry,"* she whispered, locked on the face behind the glass, soaking in the dark brow, the strong jaw-line half-hidden under a short beard. Her heart skipped a beat as her eyes held his two light brown bands celebrated by an ocean of pure white; the 'windows of the soul.' Hemera felt herself entering his soul, her hand unconsciously reaching for his face. He had a nose that, for some reason, she wanted to bite gently between her teeth. The man cleared his throat as he leaned away from her reach and gently pushed her hands away. There was a spark of static as their gloves touched.

"Very well… I am going to assume you are here with others, so I will be on my way," he said as he turned to leave. The trim cut and color of his shoulder pads unfamiliar, his first language somehow different from hers, but the human body implied underneath was unmistakable.

Human.

"*WAIT!*" Hemera yelled, suddenly panicked by the sight of the life-support on his turning back. "Wait, please! *PLEASE!*" The man had only half-turned back before the impact of Hemera's desperate hug captured him. He politely struggled a bit before stopping at hearing Hemera yell from the pain on her chest. "*OW!* You're a *h-human,* right? *Human?*" Hemera squeezed tighter. "*Oww!*"

The man tried to move back from the surprise. "Yuh, yuh… uh, I am… *hrrrgh*… you are squeezing pretty tight there, young lady." He struggled to free an arm, then patted the top of her helmet. "Are you… could you… let me go?"

Hemera fought her body, each command to release only making her muscles pull harder. Her chest objected, the fused skin screaming from the friction and pressure. Her arms finally released, but not fully letting go. She still trapped the man in a loose grip as she looked back up at the handsome face, ignoring the throb of pain over her heart. He *was* human. *Too* human. After half a year of nothing but aliens and robots, each twist and twitch of his face drowned her in subtle communications that were so clear it completely overwhelmed her.

"Looks like you have been out by yourself for a while," the man said, smiling while still politely trying to escape her grasp. "I'm guessing," he chuckled.

"I'm… sorry…" Hemera released her grip and took a step back, only to find herself stepping back in as both her arms wrapped around one of his, grabbing his thickly gloved hand in hers.

"Sorry," she said apologetically for the parts of her body that were acting on their own. "I… I'm sorry."

"OK. Let's… *ahhh…*" he sighed. "You are pretty young to be out on your own, and you are not from the *Fidela*. What is your homeship?" Something like sadness passed across his eyes and mouth as he evaluated her more.

"I'm… from… the *Konkero*." Speaking was easier as words returned to her. Her brain was remembering how to interact with humans, but thinking clearly was still a struggle: "What… can I… what… name? *Your name?*"

"You first." The man looked down, giving her a little shiver as he regarded her, then gave a sly smile, but Hemera couldn't remember her name. She sorted through her scattered thoughts like a pile of dirty laundry while an unexpectedly handsome guest leaned on the door frame.

"It's… I'm… I'm… uh… I'm… my… my *name*! Is Hemera!"

The man nodded, still trying to escape her grasp, the tiny flashes of light from their spacesuits continuing to spark.

"Hemera, nice to -"

"Hemera *Nyx!*" Hemera yelled as it came back to her. "Hemera

Nyx, from the *Imperion Konkero!*"

The man's struggling stopped, and Hemera could feel his arm pulling her in tighter, his hand deliberately gripping hers. He patted her helmet again, then left his hand there.

"I am sorry… *Hemera.* I am sorry I got upset. I know what it feels like to see another human after a long time out. I imagine you are struggling. Lots of big feelings, right?"

He gave her a moment more, then pushed her out. Putting a hard grip on her injured shoulder, he switched his grip on her hand and gave it a shake.

"Nice to meet you, Hemera Nyx." He met her eyes once more, a charming smile on his strikingly beautiful face. "My name is Sunbuck."

====== [SUNBUCK] ======

Her skin tingled as naked fingers explored his bushy eyebrows, following the curve of his cheekbones down to the square jaw, covered in soft hair, damp with perspiration. Her hands reached forward, her palms aching along his abrasive short beard as her fingers tugged on his rubbery ears.

"OK, OK, calm down. Take a breath," Sunbuck said as he gently removed her hands from his face. Hemera quietly squealed at the feeling of his exposed hands on hers, the shoulders of their spacesuits rubbing together in the tight space as they breathed each other's air.

The small transparent cube attached to the long, dingy bar was a meant for just one human-sized creature. Low-grade, short-rent rest pods were one of the most common types of services for traveling space-explorers. These simple cubes - stacked wall-to-wall around central servicing hubs - were vital for a weary creature to take a helmet off, take a nap, or even consume intoxicants; the two human occupants were only using it to talk.

"Ah, gods-*hell*, I need a drink anyway." Their helmets and gloves rested on the bar like tired puppies. Sunbuck put one of his gloves back on and tapped at the conductive buttons as he gave Hemera a sidelong glance. "Hm. I guess you could use one, too."

Hemera shrugged, still feeling the giddy electricity from their physical contact. Him agreeing to let her touch his face was a consolation: he had deliberately left the *Fidela*, a homeship like the *Konkero*, and had no idea where any other humans were. She had been so distraught at the revelation that he suggested a face-to-face, a genuine connection in a shared physical space, saying it was the least he could do. He clicked a few more times and two drink-pouches filled, the metal-mesh tubes elongating. Sunbuck twisted them off, handing one to her, then motioned to the top of his tube as Hemera reached for her helmet.

"You don't need the straw. Here. Pull back this tab. You see? Then you can drink without a helmet." He demonstrated by pulling back a small tab with his finger and taking a deep, long drink. Hemera found the tab on hers and took a long chug. The liquid didn't taste very good. It was mostly water, the sharp tang of fabricated additives that affected the nervous system almost tasteless.

The Fangs avoided intoxicants for the most part, and she never had the time to explore on her own. Still, the concept was intriguing. She'd seen deliberate intoxication affect groups of different aliens in different ways, so she had to wonder what kind of affect it would have on her.

The tight space was saturated with the aroma wafting out from the gaps around their loose neck bands. The biochemical mix, the smell of two humans who lived in their spacesuits, saturated her brain as much as the intoxicants started to do, both making her feel easier and warmer in certain places. The throbbing of her chest-wound began gently settling down as well. She took another drink, not wanting to think about when she'd have to cut her fused skin to peel her suit off. There would be a scar that would live over her heart for the rest of her life.

Sunbuck cleared his throat as he looked around. "The 'Fangs of the Void,' huh?" Bumpy alien flesh pressed against the other side of his glass wall. "Why do caravans of homeless people always pick such scary names?"

Hemera took another drink, grateful for the looseness around her neck. "It says 'back off, I can defend myself.' I think. That's how they explained it to me." She took a swig, then continued. "You know, like the Fist of Darkness, the Army of Fire, the Star-Raiders... Damn, the Star-Raiders had such a cool name."

She gulped some more liquid as she continued. "Did you know they actually didn't do any raiding? Well... other than a few times, but... well... you have to admit that the Star-Raiders had an awesome name."

Sunbuck nodded thoughtfully. "What do you do, then? How do the Fangs make money?"

Hemera took a swig. "Oh, you know," she said, wiping her mouth. "This last one, it was something like an eight-month supply run? They found me two months in, and I've been with them ever since."

Sunbuck leaned back, trying to crack his neck. "What was the cargo?"

Hemera took a good long chug, then burped. "*Sealed.* Don't ask questions."

She cast a side-eye at the man, who yawned out wide, touching both sides of the cube with his wide hands. "Sunbuck... You really don't know any way I can get back to... to *humanity?*"

His expression soured for a moment, then shifted into a dull sort of sadness. He picked up and took a small sip from his tube, then shrugged. "I am sorry Hemera, but at this point we are both equally lost in space."

Sunbuck watched Hemera take another hefty gulp, then leaned forward, half-serious. "The Fangs of the Void. Can you leave, if you want to?" He grew completely serious. "Are you being held prisoner?"

Hemera smiled and almost laughed, spilling a drop mid-gulp. "What? No! *Haha!* I'm Sub- ... hell, I'm actually their Leader!" Her wide smile slowly dropped. "...oh... *shit! Wormy!*"

Hemera shoved Sunbuck aside as she launched for her helmet and gloves, swearing to herself as she chugged the rest of her drink and fumbled with her spacesuit at the same time.

"Wait a minute. Who is..." Sunbuck objected as Hemera shoved him aside and talked quickly as she grabbed her gloves and helmet.

"Wormy is my friend and the Leader of the Fangs. And he's... I think he's some sort of king? Prince? Of a kingdom that's over one hundred thousand star systems! And he's being hunted - well, he got caught, but I just rescued him and now we're on the run and I only came down here for supplies but then I saw you and got distracted and now... can you please get your helmet on?"

Sunbuck pushed his helmet on and locked it, getting his second glove a twist before giving Hemera a thumbs-up. She slammed the release button, and the small space splashed in colorful froth before releasing in a small puff.

"Hemera, wait," Sunbuck reached for Hemera, but to his surprise she had already reached back, grabbing his hand instead.

"You wait," she said, clicking the display pad on her wrist, scrolling, then clicking again. Sunbuck's eyebrows went up at his display, but then he shrugged. Hemera's display lit up again.

```
[OUTGOING LOCATION TRANSFER]
[STATUS: SUCCESS]
```

"Slow down, Hemera. *Where* is this? Who is... *Wormy?* And *what* is going on?" Sunbuck put a restraining gloved hand on her helmet as he looked over the navigation data.

"OK, but follow me, and quickly." Hemera stepped out of the cluster of bar-pods and out into the main hallway, still thick with crowds, as she clicked on her radio. "Wormy! Are you there?" The radio was silent for a moment, then quiet murmurings came floating back.

[HEMERA NYX. *REPLY* I SEEM TO HAVE BEEN CAUGHT
IN A PATROL SCAN. *REGRET* I AM ADJUSTING MY
POSITION, BUT SHIPS ARE INBOUND. *CONCERN* WE
NEED TO LEAVE. NOW. *PANIC*]

"WHAT?! Get away from there, *now!* Just pick a direction and *go.*
I'll *find* you." Sunbuck stepped back from Hemera as she used her
whole body to reply, then turned back to him. "We need to-"

"*No.* Hemera, stop!" Sunbuck grabbed Hemera's arm and wheeled
her around, staring down at her as his grip sparked and flashed on
her arm. A clump of Knee-Looped Beaks hopped and scuttled around
them as Sunbuck bore down on her.

"Explain. *Now.*"

"OK, yeah, just... let me go..." She shifted under his grip, which he
released, apparently surprised by how hard he had grabbed her. Hemera took a step back, arms out wide. "Wormy is my friend! He's also
wanted by the Collected Alliance because he's-"

"WHAT?! Oh... you... you stupid fucking *idiot.*" Sunbuck shouted,
incredulous to the point of outraged as he stabbed her with words
that cut through her like a sword made of ice and malice. Hemera was
shocked to stillness, wholly unprepared for such a vicious insult, her
arms still outstretched.

"You are *fucked,*" Sunbuck continued as he took another step back.
He shook his head, then leaned forward, grabbing her arms and pulling them down. "Drop the alien and *run.* You have got your spaceship,
yuh? There is a justice mainframe, just there..." He pointed towards a
computer-tower at the corner of the intersection, then turned back
to look at Hemera, all the anger replaced with concern as he tapped
his forearm display, still lit with coordinates. "Turn in the location of
this... *Hideout.* Give them this *worm-man.*"

Hemera looked back in confusion, but Sunbuck shook his head at
the appraisal. "This is the only way you *might* live, Hemera Nyx. If you

do not, you are dead. You…" He released her arms and stepped back, a display of understanding unfolding across his bearded face. "You have no clue, do you? Just how big the Collected Alliance is? What kind of weapons do they have? Just how many people they can and will send to kill you?" He threw his hands up in the air. "A one hundred thousand star kingdom? It is *dust*."

He continued, pointing down hard. "We, right now, are in *C.A.* space. They operate this Outpost. All **PLOT** sockets connect to the central computer. They are going to find you, make the association, and then hunter-robots are going to come down that hallway…" he said, pointing down one end of the long street, "… to arrest you!" He stepped back away from her, pointing in the other direction. "There. Is. No. Time. Let us *go!*"

Hemera knocked her fists against her helmet as she took another step back. "I can't leave Wormy behind! He's my friend! I just risked my life to *rescue* him. I can't-"

"Yes, you ca-" Sunbuck stepped forward angrily, but then stopped, spotting something past her shoulder. Hemera quickly glanced behind her. A squad of hunter-robots, armed and searching, stamped their way down the corridor, the crowd getting agitated, shapes and figures diving for cover. She turned back.

Sunbuck was gone.

======[TELLING A STORY]======

"Annnyway, I, like, dove for cover behind these big awesome pillars, and it was all dark and light and the robots were like *'brrzz we are lookin' for you'* and I was like… bessuuu! Like that! I need, like, a *pistol…* I bet I could… I could… like… *pew pew pew!* It'd be easy…"

Hemera turned her red face back at Wormy, who had been listening intently about how and why she had become significantly intoxicated.

"Sss… ssorry for almost hitting you w-with the *Ssparrow*, Wormy."

Wormy shrugged, his calm, sober demeanor a wet blanket on Hemera's enthusiasm.

[WE SHOULD NOT RETURN TO THE HIDEOUT. *STATE-MENT*]

"Whaaa? Why not?" Hemera rolled her head in the zero gravity, nodding gently to the memory of a song that floated at the edges of her awareness.

[I HAVE DECIDED A NEW COURSE OF ACTION. *CAU-TION*]

She nodded. "I know... what you mean... I'm... just... like... I'm just a *nobody*. If you returned to your place, you could rule a hundred thousand *stars*... I don't... get it... I don't understand why that's so, so... I don't... even... a living planet, I think."

Hemera suddenly felt very heavy.

[YOU SAVED MY LIFE. *GRATEFUL* I CANNOT STOP YOU FROM RETURNING TO THE HIDEOUT. *SADNESS* YOU ARE LEADER, AND I WILL FOLLOW YOU. *RE-SPECT*]

Hemera chuckled, her eyes closed, seeing bright colors and shapes forming at the edges. Her face suddenly twisted as a single thought reached out of the void and grabbed her heart with the icy hand of death.

It shouldn't have been that easy.

[IT IS TIME FOR YOU TO BECOME THE LEADER YOU WERE MEANT TO BE. *CONVICTION*]

"Thatss *right!*" she slurred, opening her eyes a crack as she flexed her arms. "I'm a gods-damned *hero!*"

[I HAVE DECIDED TO RETURN TO MY KINGDOM. I WILL

TAKE MY PLACE. I WILL FIGHT THE COLLECTED ALLI-
ANCE. *RESOLUTION*]

"Aahhh... hah." Hemera wasn't sure how to feel about that, not
fully able to grasp abstract concepts. Her head felt weighty, thick. The
squirm of discontent in her chest twisted away every time she tried to
grab it, and it was getting difficult to keep her eyes open.

Wormy had already removed the glass tube from her pack, and
now that he had made his proclamation, he shoved and twisted the
glass tube into a connector on his suit. The somewhat-alive blob
wriggled up and down as it appeared to wake up. Hemera focused
her blurry eyes on it as it looked back at her, its dumb optical sensors
twitchy.

"... what... *is* that thing, anyway?"

He patted the tube as the blob slid gently into his spacesuit.

[NEGA-PARASITE. IT GIVES MY SPECIES/PEOPLE COM-
PANIONSHIP AS IT SLIDES/MOVES ALONG MY BODY,
PROVIDING NOURISHMENT AND DEEP INTOXICATION/FUN
UNTIL IT IS FULLY ABSORBED. *INFORMING*]

"So... it's... all *three?*" Hemera's mind was blown. "*Wow...*"

Wormy waved to her, then turned his visor to black as he clicked
off his radio. He stopped moving as a small lump began traveling
underneath his bronze suit fabric, and Hemera groused at the sudden
loneliness. It'd be another hour before they reached the right tunnel,
and Hemera couldn't shake the unknowable feeling poking at the
edges of her awareness. Something was happening behind the scenes.
The structures of power endlessly moved; love and hate, heat and cold,
light and darkness - these primordial elements threw chains across
the galaxy, binding peoples, planets, and even the stars themselves
together into chaos, beauty, and destruction.

Hemera's imagination flowed out of the *Sparrow*. The galaxy spun
in her own time, the flow of stars a rational, living speed. The sparks
from the first explosion swam in the void, themselves bursting to

life, flaring brightly only to pop, sending out waves of stuff into the nothing. Those dusty waves began pulling together, seeds of matter exploding into more suns, becoming more seeds, growing, expelling, endlessly compacting, building *density* from nothing.

Hemera shook her head, looked around, then back at Wormy, who was clearly asleep. Kicking her controls, she whispered to herself, suddenly feeling tired.

"We're getting you back to the *Hideout*. The Fangs can help us decide what to do next, from the safety of about five thousand light years away from here."

Her face set into stone as her heavy eyelids descended.

"We're going to be safe."

====== [AND THEN] ======

Beep! Beep! Beep!

"...*nurrr*..." Hemera grumbled as her hands found the button on their own, her eyes still glued shut. It took a moment of rubbing them to get them to open against the iron fatigue numbing her face.

Just ahead, the unmistakable cubic shape of the *Hideout* was expanding. Any object in the void could be any size without something to compare it to, so for a moment it seemed as if she was on a journey through size rather than distance.

Another few moments cured her of that confusion. The unmistakable outlines of *Third Hope*, *Striker*, and *Sentry* drifting outside the half-open hangar doors pulled her back to reality.

"Hey, wake up!" Hemera nudged Wormy with an elbow. He grumbled and shifted, shaking his own helmet with his arms as his visor switched back to clear. Hemera shuffled under him, reaching the radio console as they rapidly approached. "Salution, Fangs of the Void! Both of your Leaders are inbound, and..."

The *Hideout* was growing rapidly larger as they sped towards it, her relieved smile turning to a frustrated growl. "Mushroom, I told you to be ready to go!"

She released the button to a chorus of cheering, hooting, and other vocalizations that rumbled through the tinny radio, garbling her translator into chaos. Hemera couldn't help but regain her smile at the celebration. She glanced back at Wormy, all his small blue teeth on display, when the mechanical speaking of Mushroom cut through the chatter.

[IMPOSSIBLE. *CONFUSION*]

Hemera frowned at the familiar sound. "Mushroom. Why aren't we docked and locked?"

[SECONDARY HANGER DOOR/COVER IS STUCK/BROKEN, LEADER *REPORT*]

Rubbing her head in her hands, Hemera made a plan out of pure habit. "OK. Wormy, I'll drop you off at the bridge first, and then I'll see what I can do about the doors. If I use the *Sparrow's* cutter, it might be faster than trying to repair them. We really need to get the gods-hell out of here as soon as possible."

Wormy murmured the most intricate murmur Hemera had ever heard.

[EVERY FANG OF THE VOID QUESTIONED MY DECISION TO MAKE YOU SUB-LEADER. *STATEMENT* YOU KNEW NOTHING, LIKE A NEW-HATCHED LARVA. *MEMORY*]

They had covered the distance quickly, flying past *Striker* as it flashed celebratory lights. Hemera pulled up and leveled with the top of the cargo hauler, the small bridge hanger door sliding open in the distance.

"So why did you?" Hemera grunted as she twisted the *Sparrow* around, throwing the primary engine under it, going for another fast landing. One of his arms patted the top of her helmet as the thick, slowing tangles of gravitronic chains began slowing them down.

[I BELIEVED THAT YOU WERE A REAL ADVENTURER. *PRIDE* I BELIEVED THAT SOME DAY YOU MIGHT SAVE THE FANGS FROM DESTRUCTION. *PRAISE*]

Tears formed at the edges of her vision as the *Sparrow* slid inside the hanger. Her fingers clicked the landing gear as she looked back out at the glory of outer space, the endless speckle of colored lights, the entire universe itself shining down on her.

"Thank-"

The sky was now solid with the colors and trim lines of Collected Alliance warships. A thousand brilliant lasers cascading from the fronts of hundreds of warships searched, caught, and locked onto every Fang spaceship still outside the *Hideout*. There was no gap between the lock and the shot. Hyper-luminous bolts punched holes in the *Third Hope*, *Sentry*, and the still-celebrating *Striker*. A wall of flames and smoke filled the space outside, as if the void itself had caught on fire. The *Hideout* shook.

Hemera and Wormy struggled to free themselves from the tiny cockpit, then ignited their boosters, spinning, trying to orient themselves as the gravity shorted out, leaving them spinning in the air, only to be thrown against the ground as the bulbs clicked back on. Wormy wiggled all of his arms as he leveled himself and ran past the hallway door, his twin streaks from his belt pushing him forward as Hemera followed right behind.

[GET TO THE BRIDGE! *COMMAND*]

They turned to look out of the window as they rocketed down the hallway. The space around the enormous hauler was thick with Collected Alliance fighters of descending sizes, the massive warships launching spaceship transports, which launched cruisers and destroyers, which in turn launched smaller frigates and gunships.

All in frontal-attack formation, all on high alert, all headed right towards them.

A large reinforced metal-tube slammed through the hull in front of them, making them dodge the shower of sparks and shrapnel. The center of the cylinder retracted as a hunter-robot's claw gripped the edge, the sudden opening to vacuum howling.

"This way!" Hemera grabbed Wormy's arm and pulled him down the side-passage. The *Hideout* groaned and shrieked as Hemera and Wormy blasted their jets up the empty elevator shaft, making a hard curve at the top, then flaring their jets as they landed hard in the center of the bridge.

The simple announce-bot woke up, chirping loudly.

[ATTENTION: LEADER WORMY IS NOW ON THE BRIDGE]
[ATTENTION: SUB-LEADER HEMERA NYX IS NOW ON THE BRIDGE]

The bridge lit up in the lights of hunter-robots glowed attack-red. They padded around the small command hill, jagged metal teeth dripping with acid. A Collected Alliance transport had already smashed into the side of the glass dome, the rear ramp open and dark.

A single, tall, thin alien strode with a bony thoughtfulness down the ramp, the fleet of warships filling every ounce of space beyond the cracked glass dome. The alien's uniform was a bright crimson red, the golden splash of the CA logo across a shoulder, but the sight of the alien face in its helmet made Wormy stiffen upright, murmuring with an emotion Hemera had never heard before.

[YOU. *HATRED*]

====== [CAPTURED] ======

An unfurled hunter-robot pulled her arms together in a sharp, mechanical grip as it shoved Hemera roughly to her knees. A bolt-rifle barrel pressed down and smacked her helmet hard to the side. The physical statement was clear in meaning: you move, you die.

The spindly alien stepped gently down the ramp, clapping two small hands as it made some articulated human-sounding noises. Hemera was already thinking of names to call this new alien, none of them flattering.

[YOU/ENTITY DID WELL/GOOD TO HIDE/??? SO LONG/ TIME, ??? *????*]

Wormy murmured, enraged, struggling despite the gun at his head.

[INSULT/???. *HATRED*]

Hemera's blood was on fire as she tried to look around without moving her head. Two hunter-robots guarding the main door. Three above, pacing the walkways. Two more dragging a computer tower - *no, not a tower, a Justice Mainframe* - into the bridge. Her boots were still unlocked, warmed up, ready. If she flew up first, hit that one with her helmet...

[DO NOT, HEMERA NYX. THIS IS MY FIGHT. *CONVIC-TION*]

Hemera looked back at the black eye stalks. The Collected Alliance alien strode forward as it ignored Wormy's command to her, then grabbed Wormy's helmet and twisted.

[I SEE YOU STILL HAVE SOME FIGHT/SPIRIT LEFT/ OWN. *MOCKERY*]

Wormy leaned forward, leveling himself, regaining some poise against the twisting.

[YOU MOCK YOUR KING, SERF/WORM. *AGGRESSIVE*]

The bony alien bastard snapped its fingers and two hunter-ro-bots jumped behind him, upright and ready like guard dogs. Then it twisted its finger, and two more began pacing a circle around Wormy, sharp robotic teeth dripping with metalloid acid. The alien looked like

a walking pile of sticks under a thin blanket as it strode confidently,
waving a bony finger at Wormy.

[THE COLLECTED ALLIANCE IS MY KING/GOD NOW.
YOUR NOWHERE/NOTHING NO LONGER EXISTS. *STATE-
MENT*]

Wormy struggled, still held down by a robot as the thin Bony one
continued his victory gloat.

[BUT/HOWEVER, IN HUNTING YOU, I DISCOVERED YOU
HAD A NEW NOTHING. *EXPLAINING*]

The floor shook like the hangar doors had slammed shut, but
Hemera knew that couldn't be it. She held her breath in horror as a
harder vibration shook the ship more. A few sparks snapped out of
terminals.

[IT WOULD BE MORE FUN. TO NOT ONLY/JUST KILL/
END YOU. BUT EVERYONE WHO FOLLOWED YOU. YOUR
FRIENDS/FAMILY. JUST LIKE BEFORE/PAST. *SATIS-
FACTION*]

Sweat stung at the corner of Hemera's eyes as her hot, dry breath
panted on the edge of panic and despair, her brain still struggling to
process what was happening.

[TOO EASY TO LET YOU ESCAPE. YOU CAME RIGHT
BACK TO THEM. FOR MY ENJOYMENT. *HUMOR*]

At this, Wormy leaned forward, shaking hard as he murmured
loudly.

[WHY? *CONFUSION* I NEVER BOTHERED ANYONE! I
STAYED HIDDEN! *DESPAIR*]

The Bones-bastard leaned in over Wormy in a stance of ultimate
victory.

[I WAS BORED. *MOCKERY*]

At this Wormy made a noise Hemera had never heard before, a shrill kind of wailing gurgle. The robot released him as he fell wiggling onto the curved floor.

"Wormy..." Hemera turned back to the officer as he motioned to another robot, who brought up two metal sticks. Bones swung his own in a series of wide, precise swishes, then threw an identical stick down at Wormy.

[COME/URGING. I AM ON A HOLIDAY/VACATION. GIVE AMUSEMENT. *MOCKERY*]

Screaming a guttural whistling howl, Wormy launched forward, grabbing the weapon and swinging wildly for Bones' midsection. The thin, hard alien hopped back easily, parrying and countering with a thrust, but Wormy had not lost himself completely to his emotions. He leaned back hard, using his lack of bones to bend all the way around as Bones' sword stabbed the empty air. Grabbing Bones' sword with one of his upper arms, Wormy dropped his own sword to his lower arm. Hemera grit her teeth at the sound Wormy made as Bones sliced an arm off, sending a pressurized spray of liquid and air across the bridge floor, the atmosphere hissing out around the cracks in the glass.

A robot clicked and clacked as the tower flared to life.

[JUSTICE MAINFRAME IS NOW OPERATIONAL]

Bones was distracted as Wormy swung and hit the side of the chest-plate, the loud crack of metal smacking metal ringing in Hemera's ears through her radio. The red eyes of the hunter-robots flashed as they watched, ready to pounce.

Bones stepped to the side, swearing as he kicked Wormy hard, its dense mass of bone pushing deep in soft flesh, causing more biology to spray out of the wound. Wormy stumbled over a vine and howled as Bones swished again, knocking Wormy's sword from his hand. The worm-man wiggled in pain on the floor, trying to stem the bleeding and air loss. Bones regarded him for a moment longer, rubbing his chest where the sharp metal stick had nearly cut him, then stepped back, motioning to the robots as he tossed his stick aside.

[TO HIS MAJESTY'S LIST OF OFFENSES, ADD/IN-
CLUDE: ASSAULTING A GRAND SUB-LEADER. *HUMOR*]

A hunter-robot grabbed Wormy and dragged him towards the tall justice mainframe, then slammed him hard against the display. A second robot shoved a bolt-rifle hard against his helmet, while a third one extracted his **PLOT** from his spacesuit and inserted it precisely into the machine. Hemera felt the pressure of the robot pushing her down, anticipating a struggle, but all Hemera could do was watch, bewildered, catatonic. Around the edge of Wormy's visor, his eye stalks met Hemera. The only thing she could hear was the sound of his breathing in her radio as the machine clicked and processed, then flashed loudly, printing out some sort of paper covered with glyphs and barcodes. Bones, the Grand Sub-Leader, strode stiffly to the machine and plucked the paper from the printer, leaned back to read it, then nodded as it slapped the adhesive paper to Wormy's helmet.

Wormy spoke to Hemera, a final murmur escaping his long, round mouth.

[HEMERA NYX. REMEMBER YOUR PROMISE. *ACCEP-
TANCE*]

The bolt punched clean through his helmet, the spray of air and organic material blasting from both sides as his body fell limp to the floor.

Hemera couldn't move.

Then she looked up, locking eyes with those horrifying split-kind of optical sensors, bands of lights and darks, impossible to tell where they were looking - even past her own skin, seeing something deeper as it leaned in.

[AND YOU, SMALL THING/ALIEN. YOU WERE THE ONE
TO REPORT? *QUESTION*]

The question didn't make any sense. Hemera gaped like a fish out of water, her mind numb, dislocated. Bones nodded as it tapped her shoulder with a hard hand.

[YOU SEE THE UNIVERSAL TRUTH: VIOLENCE IS POWER. *LECTURE*]

Hemera grit her teeth. "I'd never betray Wormy. I'm the one who rescued him, you... you..." Hemera felt flecks of spit at the edges of her mouth as she tried to think of something, some way to strike back. "Your 'power' blinds you to your weakness, Grand Sub-Leader."

Taken aback by the rebuttal, the Grand Sub-Leader leaned in closer and blinked.

[WHAT WEAKNESS? *QUESTION*]

One of the robots dragged Wormy's limp corpse and tossed it roughly into a corner of the bridge. Grand Sub-Leader tipped its head.

[DID YOU JUST/ONLY SAY THAT TO SOUND COOL/SCARY? *QUESTION*]

She looked around once more. The impossibly tough hunter-robots, the alien eyes boring down on her, the edge of the sharp metal stick just beyond reach, Wormy's body, tossed into the corner. The pile of fabric, metal, and glass looked just like it had that first day. Her first contact, her leader, her friend.

The Fangs of the Void. The band of alien outcasts and refugees who had saved her, given her power, purpose, and companionship, now used their burning spaceships to celebrate the complete victory of their enemies. Her eyes were too blurry to work, her throat raw, face wet with sweat, tears, and snot as she prostrated herself on the floor among the dying plant matter, her suit still stiff.

"*Yes.* P-please spare me, honorable Grand Sub-Leader. *Reganto.*"

The alien scoffed, then motioned to the robots.

======[AUTOMATED JUSTICE]======

The hunter-robot brought Hemera's helmet down on the display so hard her visor cracked, a thin jagged bolt of lightning suddenly connecting the top and bottom of the glass.

She held her breath.

The glass held.

Her eyes focused on the screen in front of her, her body being held down, the press of the bolt-rifle against her tight neckband. A third robot yanked her **PLOT** out of her chest-socket and inserted it into the console. There was a beep, and the electronic display started scrolling.

============
[THE COLLECTED ALLIANCE]
[SOVEREIGN GALACTIC GOVERNMENT AUTO-JUSTICE
MAINFRAME]
[VER. 0.28B]
============
[NEW CASE FILE: F-OB-H31T61]
[STATUS: OPEN]
============
[PERSON: HEMERA NYX]
[AFFILIATIONS: SPACE TEETH]
============
[PROCESSING CRIMES]
============
...[...]...[...]...[...]...
============
[UNLICENSED SALVAGE]
[FAILURE TO PAY TOLLS]
[TRESPASSING]
[TAMPERING WITH SECURITY HARDWARE]
[PROPERTY DESTRUCTION]
[EVADING CAPTURE]
[ASSAULTING AN OFFICER]
[SMUGGLING]

[DATA THEFT]
[UNREGISTERED VEHICLE]
[MISUSE OF GOVERNMENTAL VEHICLES]
[UNSETTLING APPEARANCE]
[UNCOOPERATIVE ATTITUDE]
============
[PROCESSING PUNISHMENT]
============
... [...] ... [...] ... [...] ...
============
[PUNISHMENT]
[DEATH: ARENA]
============
... [...] ... [...] ... [...] ...
============
[REWARD INPUTS]
[REPORTING UNLICENSED SETTLEMENT]
[CAPTURING HOSTILE NATIONAL LEADER]
============
[UPDATING PUNISHMENT]
============
... [...] ... [...] ... [...] ...
============
[PUNISHMENT]
[PRISON: TRASH-HEAP]
[LABOR WEIGHT: 800000 KG]
[SHIP STORAGE: APPROVED]
============
[UPDATE CASE FILE: F-OB-H31T61]
[STATUS: CLOSED]
============

The Grand Sub-Leader sighed in disappointment as he read the adhesive paper, then slapped it to her helmet as it motioned to the robots.

[WHAT ARE WE/US, IF NOT A NATION/KINGDOM OF LAWS? *DISMISSAL*]

She should have felt something. There had been a moment where she was sentenced to death, only to be saved by the rewards for actions she never took, and she felt *nothing*.

Reporting? *Capturing?*

She couldn't feel the rough robot claw gripping her arm as it locked her into a restraining prisoner-seat. In a dream-like haze, she saw herself being dragged off of the bridge, towards a barouche, one just like... she had just found it there... the easily disabled security robot...

She looked up as the hunter-robots shoved her seat towards the cruiser, the Grand Sub-Leader taking a final victory lap as he taunted Wormy's body. Hemera had lead the Collected Alliance right to them. It must have been her, *somehow*. She was the one who brought the Collected Alliance to the *Hideout*.

Everyone was dead, and it was all her fault.

She eyed the crack on her visor as there was a final thud as the *Sparrow* impounded in the back of the barouche, then the unmistakable pull of the ship accelerating, the buzzing shield readying for tunneling.

The sole survivor of the Fangs of the Void bent in her restraints to see the floating, flaming ruins of her tribe, drifting like stars across the alien galaxy.

<u>INTERREGNUM:</u>

FILE: HEMERA NYX, IN HER OWN TIME!
TIME: 12045:12:21:23:45
LOCATION: THRONE HALL; FIRST COMMAND SPIRE;
IMPERION KONKERO

Elena Martelo, Reganto of the Imperion Alianco and Sovereign of the *Imperion Konkero*, frowned on her impressive throne of starlight-sparkled plastic.

Unsteady fingers reached the lighting panel. A quick switch and thin, curved gold-plated petals furled inwards like flowers retreating from an icy wind. More of the endless starlight flowed in, illuminating the Throne Hall in a way that could only be described as 'magical.'

Elena, however, felt like she had been shoved into a glass coffin and buried in frosty death. The pinpoints of light from the cosmos made her stomach churn, and the view it illuminated made the bile rise to the back of her throat.

Fortresses, each with their Estro couple, sat in tall-backed chairs at the edge of the primary dais. Behind them were family, business people, religious advocates, and every slimy sentima who wanted something from her, endlessly clawing at the edges of her attention, whining for favors.

Well-lit on the central dais, the stiffly dressed Leader Scribe, an ancient pile of moldy flesh propped up in a starched ceremonial suit, continued to read the proclamation through the soft music of gentle strings. The Fortresses shifted, yawned, and otherwise tried to ignore the sudden shift in light.

"… data recovery… remains stalled… due to the backup computer's power… *situation*. The location… of the Earth remains… lost… along with nearly all… of our travel logs…" The Leader Scribe nodded as they drifted off for a moment, then snapped back to reading.

"However… given the fact that the… Earth was ruled… no longer habitable… upon departure… it was determined… that data recovery efforts… to find the Earth amounted… to be nothing… more than a… vanity project… among the research… staff. The project has… been backlogged… against more… pressing concerns…"

The assembled noble-peoples and various other parasites that filled the Throne Hall made noises of discontent at the report. Elena felt her stomach gurgle in nausea. The sound of those wet sacks of meat vocalizing their… they're…

Elena grit her teeth.

Disgusting.

Her top eyelid twitched. The Leader Scribe gave a few phlegmy hacks as they shuffled handwritten papers, then gulped greedily from a wooden mug before continuing.

"Regarding recent… rioting… in the –"

The Reganto shifted and pushed the weight of her helmet-crown to her other hand, the half-mask faceplate uncomfortably warm against her cheeks. The heavy, sludgy feeling in her head grated against her nerves. The weight of her ceremonial battle armor felt like it was bending her bones.

"- dedicated security corridor… down the Grand Promenade… will help get the… the *Squads*… where they need to be… faster. Additionally… the increased number of dead zones… will be… re-purposed -"

Security. The Reganto rolled her head and looked the Leader Guard over: a powerful man, scarred and graying, the lines of hatred carved on his face like stone. *There* was a man who knew his place. He obeyed any order, and even stood by for all the… *extravagances* the Reganto occasionally enjoyed. The advancement of human sciences didn't have to be so *boring*, especially when it came to testing limits of pain and endurance. More than a few negrava had found those limits as Elena did her research, but the man's steely gaze was focused and *obedient*. She could trust him to put down the worms, to restore *sanity* to her spaceship.

Leader Scribe droned on. "- only… eighty-nine percent finished… with repairs from… the alien attack. Production… of the final panels… has been difficult due to… a lack of workers… and -"

Very much unlike Taw, Battleax, Lions, and Nyx. The Fortresses had their uses governing the sprawling empire of the Imperion Alianco, but cooped up in this deathtrap they had become nothing more than troublemakers. Her sour gaze swept the putrid lot before her, the smell of rot wafting up nauseating more as the sharp taste of bile filled her mouth.

Elena fiddled with her switches and knobs. Dimming the room, she refocused the pattern of lights on the Fortresses sitting in their sections on the floor below her. It shone brightest on each Estro and their partner, then faded gently backwards, to the seats filled with children, relatives, and merchant representatives, their dark outlines disappearing into the gloom. Elena felt a tug of her lips slightly upwards at the empty seat next to Lenna Nyx.

"- also stalled due to difficulty finding… commoners with the appropriate medical… training to -"

Commoners were only allowed in the sacred Throne Hall for entertainment, and more rarely, for the passing of judgment. Of course, what could be more entertaining that watching a *negrava* piss itself under the restrained wrath of the embodied nation known as the Reganto Imperion?

Elena tried to remember what Lenna's… *servant* looked like as she imagined him standing in the judgment ring. She could almost see his curly hair matted with dried blood, open mouth shocked at the power of the Imperion, head mounted on one of the iron spikes that decorated the front of the Reganto's quarters. The look on Lenna's face as the Reganto passed judgment on her… *lover*… would be a long-overdue thrill. Her frail heart beat faster as she remembered the dark red blood flowing down Lenna's face, the cruel slashes crossing just above her nose, the final gift from Elena's brother.

Estro Taw interjected, using the shift in lighting as an opportunity to speak. An artificially large and sleek black beard flowed from his chin onto his table, highlighting his bald head and gray, unkempt eyebrows as he gestured with full self-importance.

"What of criminal labor? The Imperion's prisons are full to bursting!"

The Leader Scribe stumbled. "Uh… yes… Estro…"

"Then send them in! Put them to use! Commoners are only here, on board, for *labor*. That should go triple for criminals… even criminal *doctors*," Estro Taw spat as he cast a side-smirk at Fortress Nyx.

Lenna's frown remained stone.

The eldest Nyx boy smiled a secret whisper back at his siblings, who then failed to hold back chuckles. They quieted as they felt the Reganto's stone gaze upon them, then fell into complete obedience as Lenna slowly turned towards them.

Elena closed her eyes as Estro Taw continued to bully the Leader Scribe, his spindly spouse clearly in a drug-induced tranquility. The mud in her mind had been swirling, and now, just when she felt like she was about to lose her mind, the thick sludge of confusion gave way to a wonderful, almost spiritual form of lightness that touched her shoulders as it rose up through her head.

She had never felt more *sane*.

The thick jungle of courtly politics and intrigue were being laid bare, the difficulties of ruling an overpopulated continent on Earth reduced, distilled into its purest expression.

It would come down to a naked display of violence, and soon. There was no other way. The 'red badges' were everywhere. Plotting. Hiding. Even in this very room. The insurgents and their army of supporting peasants would not stop unless someone *stopped* them.

Elena's hand gripped the hard plastic armrest as she imagined smashing the skulls of every human being on the ship.

The Leader Scribe shifted, then continued. "Estro… Taw… that's unfortunately… not possible… with the current… laws. Many of our current pris… criminals are… repeat… offenders. After a… third caning… or imprisonment… they lose the… right to labor."

Estro Battleax leaned back, entering the conversation with a snort of contempt from his wide, smooth face. His spouse had perfected the art of being small and timid, and Elena often did not realize she was there at all.

"Well that sure sounds like an easy life on a spaceship, doesn't it?" Battleax dramatically rose to his feet. "Is there any wonder we're losing provisions while our productivity is in the toilet?"

Battleax looked around again, more color in his round cheeks. "They've been smuggling food. They've been *breeding!* Then they commit *crimes,* so they don't have to work! Aren't we all just suckers? Why do we allow parasites to thrive aboard *our* spacecraft?"

Taw replied excitedly, bushy eyebrows jumping. "The only way we'll be able to survive is through *sacrifice.* Let them redeem themselves with their labor," he said as he nodded to Battleax, both old men of the same mind. "I move all criminals, regardless of status, be put on the highest-hour rotations for all Imperion labor."

Estro Lions had stirred from her half-slumber, only vaguely aware of the conversation. She spoke softly and slowly; the starlight frosting her white hair with sparkles of blue, yellow, and red. No one was sure if she was addressing the assembly or the even-older gentleman who was absolutely asleep next to her.

"I thought we were lacking for workers…" Lions tapped at a display pad as she became more lively. "… but it says here that our commoner population has grown since the alien attack?" She looked around, bewildered. "How does that… work?"

Lenna's voice projected smoothly and quickly. "I believe they are called *children*, Estro Lions. Do you mean to put toddlers to work on the glass furnaces?"

"Enough!" The Reganto cawed. And just in time, she thought - let Lenna Nyx talk long enough and you'd find yourself agreeing that no one needed to work at all. She growled under her half-mask as she readjusted herself aggressively in her plastic chair. "Glass output will continue as fast as it can with the workers we have. *Moving on.*"

Lenna's hand went up.

Elena growled. *Of course* Lenna Nyx was ready to move on, to bring up her pet project of trying to reinstate the Leader Public. She knew the answer was no. Asking over and over was a pointless waste of time.

The Reganto's snarl turned into a smile as she settled back into her molded plastic chair of state, sweeping her hand in a royal fashion as she motioned to the back of the room, a side-eye locked on Lenna.

"New business? You. In the back. What do you want?"

=======

The Fortress Conclave *had* to end.

At first it had been new business. The Reganto called on anyone who raised their hand, addressing or dismissing concerns at her whim. Every other hail answered, the Reganto called in the acts. It had been years since she had called on her actors and musicians. The long delay in their scrambling to fulfill her calls were worth it alone.

Lenna's hand remained upright; visible, and ignored.

The royal band stumbled together for a full rendition of the national war-chant. All twenty-three minutes of it. As she was the pure embodiment of what they were praising, the Reganto remained in her throne as everyone else stood to sing along.

Next, the scriptures. The rhyming chants of the Divine Journey of the Goddesses was a monotonous, droning kind of hymn. It filled the throne room with a sonic buzz that nearly put everyone to sleep.

Then the dancers. Trying and failing to amp up the room with their spins and leaps, only a

scattering of applause sprinkled back at them
through the yawning and low conversations filling the back of the hall.

Jugglers.

Mimes.

Then a disagreement among the Fortresses on the protocols of making motions to end
a Fortress Conclave, which spiraled into the
Sub-Leader Research's aids rushing to find specific books deep in the Library, which was then
followed by an ad hoc agreement to re-address
the issue at a later date.

Then a girl only a few years from being in
her own time bravely took the central dais and
recited the first third of 'The Founding of Fortress Lions' before forgetting the rest and
running off in tears.

Estro Taw, seeing an opening to talk,
launched into a substantially incoherent airing
of grievances covering the width and breadth of
the spaceship: bemoaning the suspicious taste
of lab-grown food, denouncing the general attitude of the commoners aboard, whining about
the gravity bulbs made everyone feel a little
chilly no matter how hot the air was.

Then the mimes returned, even though no one
had asked them to.

It had been more than three hours. Elena
could see it in their eyes: the suspicions, the
hatred, the plotting. Bladders and hemorrhoids
flaring and spasming. Lenna's hand remained upright throughout; a numb, unyielding post,
half-hidden behind the unreasonable amount of

mimes occupying the dais.

Elena smiled under her golden half-mask, the weight of the helmet-crown trying to pull her head down as she watched the silent, bendy idiots amuse the infantile morons.

The Reganto cleared her throat. "Leader Scribe?"

The Leader Scribe wobbled back to their feet and bowed stiffly. "*Gloro de Servo,* Reganto... Under your command... we end..."

Lenna Nyx jumped to her feet, her dead hand slamming loudly on her wooden desk.

"*Reganto Imperion!* We have a final matter to discuss!"

The Throne Hall dropped to silence.

Estro Nyx had halted a royal command.

Elena fought the small smile that tugged at the edges of her mouth. Stuck-up, self-righteous, stubborn, the shield of pride the negrava-tainted *Nyx* held in their chests bothered her far more than the fiery pain she had from sitting for too long.

"My third child. Hemera, of Fortress Nyx." Estro Nyx motioned as her youngest daughter stood up and walked stiffly to the central dais. A grumble of tired, angry sentima sitting back in their seats filled the hall.

The girl was everything Elena Martelo despised about the Nyx family. Rolled into a formal braid, her deeply-colored hair the color of sunset so richly saturated it seemed unnatural. Her ruddy complexion was dotted with dark freckles, and her large mouth seemed practiced in both smiling and scowling. And those strange eyes. A swirling mix of green and brown, so shiny they seemed to produce their own light, staring right back at her with undisguised loathing.

The teenager bowed in her deep, earthen-blue overalls. Swooping an arm gracefully up, then down, then both forward and back, the teenager regained only a sliver of personal pride in the final, humbled position: the ornate ceremonial bow of someone meeting the Reganto Imperion for the very first time.

Elena had expected a sloppy attempt, thick with resentment and the mockery of youth, but a little shiver ran up her back at the sight. That kind of precision, grace, fluidity… that could only come from hours of practice. There was no denying it. The bow had been *exactly* right. The Reganto's teeth grit at the realizations that someone had been teaching this child powerful things, but the edges of her frown soon tipped upwards again. The peasants would get what was coming to them, but maybe… maybe it was time for a naked display of violence against the Fortresses themselves?

Lenna saluted, calling out in a clear, proud voice that saturated the Hall. "Fortress Nyx humbly requests the Reganto Imperion to acknowledge Hemera in her own time."

Lenna bowed deeply and, perhaps for the first time in her life, it seemed as if she really meant it.

Elena's head bent back slightly as the epiph-
any tapped her skull like a crystal bell.

It was madness.

=======

Madness. Of *course.*

Elena swore to herself for not seeing it
sooner. The alien attacks, the rioting, the
loss of the Earth, all this time crammed up in
this hideous glass spaceship lost in the middle of nowhere. It was all too much for their
small, fragile minds to handle.

Imaginary monsters living in the tunnels.
Conspiring to return to the very-dead Earth.
Labor strikes. *Unionizing.* And now, demanding
recognition for this… this *negrava*, the one responsible for so much damage, as a *sentima?*

The Reganto fought back rage as she fiddled
with the small panel of knobs and buttons on
the side of her armrest. The room darkened as
ceiling petals unfurled. The girl Hemera now
sparkled with starlight from nearly every direction, only slightly less brilliant than the
Reganto herself. The mottled starlight on her
saturated hair was luminescent, each loose
strand topped with a dot of colored light. A
small shiver ran down Elena's spine again, and
her eyes widened softly as she sat up on her
throne.

"Mmmm… the famous *Hemera* and her… *fist of justice!*"

The girl remained steel against the Reganto's
mockery.

"Inciting a riot, was it? What were the numbers again?"

The teenager's eyes turned to glass as she
immediately replied. "Reganto. Two hundred seventy-four injured. Eighty-six missing. Twelve
dead. Reganto."

"You could imagine what would have happened
to you if you weren't a child." Elena smiled to
herself, becoming a bit more animated in her
chair. "Guilty of treason, perhaps? I wonder…"

Could they not *see* it? The Agreements said
it clearly: the responsibility of the disci-
pline of an Estro's child fell to the Estro,
not the Reganto. That was the only reason Elena didn't string little Hemera up by her guts
on the Grand Promenade that very day. And yet,
here they were, asking - *begging* - for the only
protection this girl had to be taken away.

They were *insane*.

Elena felt her teeth grind as her jaw set
hard. She fought against her mind as it filled
with plans, trying to calm herself. There was
time to do it *right*. No more impediments, no
more sabotage. Curing the *Imperion Konkero* from
the disease of space madness was Elena Martelo's true destiny.

The Reganto Imperion rolled her head to the
other side, feeling contempt for the illuminated child that played no part in her new plans.
Perhaps, for fun, a swipe of the claw.

"Tell me, child. Are you a sentima, or a *negrava*?"

That shut them up. The gossipers in the back, the bored children, the murmurings of advisers under breath. All were suddenly quiet as the Reganto's poisonous scowl switched into an enthusiastic smile under the half-mask.

Wouldn't it be something if she had Hemera Nyx executed on the spot?

No, she chided herself. *She's not a Nyx yet.*

The silence had given way to muttering, with some vocal objections from the assembly at the slur, but more than a few guffaws also scattered about. Taw and Battleax served up their ass-kissing chuckles with gusto, while Estro Lions seemed to struggle to keep up with what was happening as she asked quiet questions to no one in particular.

Lenna's daughter tilted her head back at the Reganto. The oinking of the swine did not penetrate the Reganto's thoughts as she focused on Lenna Nyx's scarred face. Red and solid like heated iron. Then, slowly, giving way to full panic at the sign of her daughter squaring her shoulders. The girl Hemera's voice was strong and confident in her reply.

"That's the same question the boy asked me, right before I broke his nose."

Hemera's eyes were bright multi-colored searchlights seeking the Reganto's, hidden as they were in the dark behind the half-mask of her crown.

"My answer's the same, *Reganto*."

The Reganto Imperion laughed. The burst of
chuckling gave way to honking and wheezing as
she gripped her fragile sides. The collective
breath in the room released, some joining in
with polite laughter. Hemera's mother was pale,
breathing shallow panic breaths, an apology
written across her x-scarred face that, perhaps, surprised Elena more than little Hemera's
suicidal insult. The Reganto's laughter faded as a smile tugged at the edges of her royal mouth, the wet taste of venom seeping in the
edges of her dry, cracked lips.

"You may well wish for the days of childhood,
when insulting the Imperion Itself could be so
easily forgiven."

Hemera stood her ground for a moment, then
bowed her head. Elena leaned back, regulat-
ing this teen-aged difficulty to be dealt with
at some later date. There was a more pressing
problem to attend to: tens of thousands of her
citizens had lost themselves to madness. The
infected, the rotted, the irredeemable… there
was no saving them. To save the *Konkero,* those
taken by the space madness had to be *inciner-
ated* down to the very last scrap of flesh and
bone.

The core of the spaceship was hot enough.

The Reganto swept her hand in the gesture of
a blessing as she proclaimed:

"The Reganto Imperion recognizes Hemera of
Fortress Nyx in her own time."

The traditional pause, then the motion of invitation.

"Declare your service."

Hemera of Fortress Nyx stood up straight as a board, and with a strong, swift motion, she tapped her forehead and then her shoulder while calling out her praise of service to the Imperion.

"*Gloro de Servo!*"

The Reganto nodded in approval. "Hemera Nyx," Elena said as she added a final tightening of the chains. "May you live a life of *endless* adventure."

The chamber rolled into the traditional coming-of-age cheer, with some Fortresses less than enthusiastic. Elena relaxed, letting a hissing sigh of relief escape her lips as she sunk back into the synthetic throne. It was time for every human being aboard her ship to remember who was in charge. The homeship's core would feed on the insane and grow stronger from the nourishment. Only the sane would remain, freed from the taint of evil and cured from their derangements.

In the warm light that flowed from the Reganto Imperion, everything would be made right. The Parade of Progress would continue to bring enlightenment to the galaxy.

The young Hemera smiled a bright, charming smile as she left the dais and ran back to Fortress Nyx, embracing her family in an informal manner, hugging and high-fiving like the insane, filthy subhuman scum they were. The Reganto let her heavy crowned-helmet nod for her as she watched the Nyx family celebrate. The simple policy change had cleansed her mind and spirit,

the new path forward as brilliant as it would
be effective: *kill them all.*

   The Reganto leaned forward like a crane about
to strike, the celebratory spirit evaporating
in the sudden cold as her voice cut through the
cheers.

   "*So!* Hemera… *Nyx.* My good young *lady.* I have…
situations to attend to, but! *We* still have a
moment. Was there something… you wanted to say
to me? Something… you needed to get off your
chest…"

   Hemera's head bowed, eyes lowered on the
thick woolen carpet, her mouth hard-shut. The
Throne Hall was so quiet the attendants in the
back could hear the smirk grow across the Reganto's face.

   "*…hm?*"

   Elena caught Lenna's gaze as she turned to
gloat, but Estro Nyx's obedience had vanished.
Those once-vacant pupils were flames, the unbroken stare a promise of action, the feral rage
of a mother protecting her child. Right then
and there, if need be.

   "*Feh,*" the Reganto Imperion said as her smirk
dropped. She didn't need to fight Lenna or Fortress Nyx. In her charity and compassion, the
Reganto let them have their brief victory. It
didn't matter.

   Elena's naked feet would blacken with the
char and ashes of the dead. Her army of loyal
followers would be her own body and mind. Everything would be like it was supposed to be.

It would start *now*.

Elena Martelo, Reganto of the Imperion Alian-co and Sovereign of the *Imperion Konkero*, is-sued her command as the Throne Hall filled with light. It was a statement of victory over the firewood that filled her court, dangling by the strings she herself would cut, one by one, into the fires of the *Konkero's* heart.

"This Fortress Conclave is dismissed."

The cosmic ballet of creation and destruction continues, and our hero is in the way! Can she escape from her hellish prison and find a way to safety? Or is it already *too late?!*

Hemera Nyx
Space Adventurer

In...

THE EFFULGENT RECRUDESCENCE!

```
=======
[TIME: 12048:08:01:02:48]
=======
[LOCATION: TRASH-HEAP]
[PRISON #TTGL-OP-126]
=======
[STATUS: INCARCERATED]
=======
```

======= **[CORE INSTABILITY]** =======

Somewhere just beyond a far-flung corner of the galaxy, a star six hundred thousand times brighter than the Sun is almost out of fuel.

The unimaginable radiance of such an intense hyper-giant made natural planetary formation impossible. It was a testament to the power of life, then, that beyond such impossibilities an *artificial* planet orbited.

Hundreds of millions of years of alien industries did what industries do: turn useful raw materials into useless junk. That useless junk, from small household wastes to derelict space stations, had been dumped and forgotten like dust in the corner of a home. The eons of dumping had consolidated and compressed as gravity molded these wastes into a geologically active and life-rich sphere suffocated by endless churning clouds of oil and colored gases: it became the planet called Trash-Heap.

The jagged surface of this rubbish-orb was criss-crossed with mountains of junked spacecraft, jagged peaks covered in frozen and slushy poison. Small oceans of ancient fuels lapped at dissolved shores, spreading caustic miasma across the the shadows of the perpetual twilight. The metal ground of Trash-Heap was dotted in huge tree-like spikes, each centered in its own small impact crater where they had been dropped from orbit.

On one of these structures a tiny figure sat swinging small legs in the toxic air, unaware of the collapsing star pressurizing towards cosmic annihilation.

======= **[DESPAIR]** =======

Hemera Nyx closed her eyes as she pulled her ratty orange-trimmed green cloak's hood farther over her stained, cracked helmet. There was nothing much to see over the edge of the tower, even as a few other towers drifted in and out of view through the haze. She let her legs dangle off the edge of the *Sparrow's* cockpit as she tried to work through the restless discontent, fighting her interior war. Halfway between crying and yelling, she glanced up at the scraps of metal and broken technologies that drifted slowly upwards. The bits of electronics and metal chunks were pulled by the gravity-magnets of the Observer, the orbiting processing station that pulled useful materials mined deep underground.

Past the drifting detritus, the microscopic dot of a star so far away it barely warmed the planet hung like a luminescent grain of sand. It was bright enough to cause the working half her visor to darken despite its tiny size.

Or, it used to. Hemera frowned as she blinked one eye and then the other. The strip of repair tape that ran down the glass separated the two slightly different shades. There was no denying that the sun was getting less bright. Or perhaps it was her mood that darkened. She leaned back as she let her legs dangle off the cockpit, watching the scrap floating higher, her gloved fist absentmindedly knocking on the glass of the *Sparrow* below her. Only a hint of wind whistled through the vista of broken glass and rusted holes.

The same orbital Observer that endlessly extracted their mining efforts would tag her engine and punt an energy beam through her spaceship before she could break atmosphere. She'd seen it happen: the powerful pink beam rippling down from the sky, the angry orange explosion. The memory of that prisoner's fail escape haunted her, even as it was just another memory to add to the collection of horrors and traumas she'd picked up over the years.

Years? She raised a heavy arm.

======

[TIME: 12048:08:01:03:06]

======

Just over a year since she woke up injured and without her memory. Or several lifetimes, from how it felt. Her eyes drifted with the scrap, higher and higher, knowing something up there was looking back at her. She wondered when her birthday was. As her eyelids started to close she saw a long brown face, four eye stalks looking back at her, pleading, extracting a promise…

And then a dozen unblinking red eyes stared back at her through a forest of short, spiky hair. Long hinged pincers that clicked their metal sheathes as thick, twitching legs thudded around her.

[PREY FOUND. *SUCCESS*]

Hemera smiled sadly at the giant spider and stretched her achy shoulder. "Hey Araneo. What's going on?"

[I WONDERED WHERE YOU HAD GONE. *CONCERN*]

The spider gave Hemera a playful sparking tap on her helmet with one of his large legs, then shook her shoulder with one of his finger-covered pedipalps as he settled next to her on the pile of space-ships. Hemera cast a concerned glance at the spider as he took in the unappealing view. His clear, rounded visor was still in relatively good shape, but his spacesuit… it had started off as a dark rubbery kind of fabric, but by this point it had become a patchwork of tape and other ad-hoc fixes.

[OUR STAR DIMS MORE/FARTHER. *QUIZZICAL* SITUA-
TION IS A CONCERN. *WORRY*]

"Araneo, let me see that," Hemera said as she tapped one of his clawed metal booties. He gently lifted his leg as Hemera darkened the working half of her cracked visor more, lifting her free hand to cover the clear broken side.

Welding the metal hook that protected the end of his segmented spider-leg, Hemera evaluated the rest of his metalwork. The dents and rust were getting worse, and she spotted yet another new strip of repair tape along the tibia of a back leg.

"Maybe it's a metaphor for how much life on this planet sucks." She handed him his leg back with an affectionate pat. Her space-suit wasn't far behind. Working on a planet made almost entirely of rusted metal and broken glass was hell for any kind of protective suit. The beautiful blue had faded and browned at the edges, the pollutants

slowly percolating past her electro-static protection, endlessly eroding and dissolving everything, everywhere.

Araneo looked down at her and tapped on the top of his helmet.

[METAPHORS ARE NOT… *INCOMPLETE* THIS IS REAL
LIFE. *STATEMENT*]

"Mm." She lightened her visor to see her reflection in the spider's
shiny visor staring back at her. The passionate flash in her reflected eyes were too bright to meet, so she let her gaze fall. Her hands
twitched hard, then relaxed to stillness.

[I HAVE A GIFT FOR YOU. *AFFECTION* PERHAPS IT
WILL ELEVATE YOUR SPIRITS. *HOPE*]

He fiddled with a pouch for a moment, then pulled something out
and dropped it into her open hands. It was a rock about the size of
her fist. Smooth, deeply colorful in a sort of rich, liquid rainbow that
shifted colors as she turned it over in her hands, the dull light saturating it until it almost seemed to glow. Something about it reminded
her of sugar, sweetness… *candy*.

"*Ah!*" Her eyelid twitched as a flood of memories of sweets came
back. Smacking her mouth together, feeling the slimy chunks stuck
to her teeth with her tongue, she swore softly to herself, vowing once
again to stop *remembering*. Memories of delicious treats assaulted her
mind, her body in open revolt. The *taste…*

"*Oohhhfff…*" she said, sitting down under that weight, trying to
breathe through it, feeling the water at the edges of her eyes. "This is
the *worst*."

[YOU DO NOT LIKE THE GIFT? *REGRET*]

Hemera looked up at the apologetic spider. "No, I do like it. I really do. It just reminded me of… something." The colorful rock called
her attention back. A gloved finger traced several small scratched
symbols, the rough cuts marring the smooth surface. She tried to
appreciate how pretty it was despite her sudden salivating.

Without thinking, her hand pressed it against the glass of her helmet, trying in vain to lick it, only to catch the flash of the crack in her glass. She sucked angrily on her water-straw, unable to wipe the corners of her frustrated mouth as shoved the rock into a pouch.

"Thank you, Araneo. It's beautiful." Hemera smiled back up at her friend as she secured the rock in a pouch on her belt, then shifted uncomfortably in her spacesuit. The thick oily buildup on her skin was really starting to get to her, but the smell was far worse. The stink of the planet seeped past her electro-static shield and saturated the rubber bits of her spacesuit. That life-threatening fetor mixed with the unwashed funk from her suit's insides, causing a nauseating miasma that saturated her air cycling system no matter how many times she expelled the exhaust.

Araneo leaned closer, vocalizing softly. It was a bubbling, chirping noise, punctuated occasionally by clicks and snaps of the hinged, metal-covered fangs. His dozen eyes tracked her calmly as he nearly touched his glass to hers, his short pedipalps folded under his head.

[WHAT WILL YOU DO WHEN/AFTER YOU ARE FREE? *CONCERN*]

Hemera continued to look up. Slow conveyor belts and buckets pulled more salvage up the trunk of the tower - each one a small success for the other miners below. Araneo shuffled, lowering his sternum closer to the ground, his short forelegs mindlessly shuffling debris.

[WE SHOULD LEAVE THIS PLANET. *SADNESS*]

"Ha," Hemera said, a small smile tugging at the edges of her eyes. "Well, the *Sparrow* is ready to go," she said, giving the cockpit window a slap. "How are you getting out?"

Araneo waved a leg at the pile of spaceships they sat on.

[MANY OF THESE SPACESHIPS ARE STILL OPERATIONAL. *STATEMENT* THE ONLY WORRY IS THE ORBITAL

SECURITY BEAM. *FRUSTRATION*]

She sat up, feeling a little anger rising inside. "Even if you made it past the lasers, you'd still be tagged an escaped fugitive. I've seen what the Collected Alliance is capable of. You'd have ten thousand hunters after you for the rest of your life."

Araneo's jaws snapped.

[I WOULD PREFER THAT TO THIS. *PLOTTING*]

Hemera sat up completely and rested the edge of her helmet on her knees, trying not to think of the void erupting into a sea of flames, the solid mass of warships killing everyone she cared about. She tried to not remember whose fault it was.

Time passed as the two friends sat in silence. Eventually, an internal pressure stirred a memory, a motivation, the reason she here in the first place.

"I need to use the rest-pod."

[YOU BELIEVE THE REST-PODS AT THE TOP ARE SUPERIOR? *QUESTION*]

"Well, all the stuff gets extracted from the tubes and pipes underground, right? They get processed up the trunk, so the stuff in the top pods should be the best."

[OVERUSE IS WHY THE TOP REST-PODS ARE THE ONES THAT BREAK MOST OFTEN. *STATEMENT*]

"I thought the tower was actually alive and killed prisoners it doesn't like?" Hemera smirked and jumped off the *Sparrow* as she waved for the arachnid to follow. "Come on. My electro-static armor is acting up again, and we'll dissolve if we spend too much time out here."

Human and space-spider began their way across the large, flat platform towards the gaping hole in the center, cast in shadow from the enormous metal cover that sat supported, ready and waiting to seal the tunnel for good.

====== [CORE COLLAPSE] ======

The alchemy of nature working a hundred million years of magic in the threshold between matter and energy came to an abrupt end as the last of the free hydrogen compressed into helium. The star, no longer pushing itself out with the radiance of cosmic nuclear fusion, gave way to the irresistible pull of gravity. The sudden inrush of matter crunched into a critical mass of pressure.

For a nanosecond, the once-brilliant star compressed into absolute dark: the unexpressed form of pure existence. Purity itself.

From that darkness a photonic detonation snapped. It was so bright it would eventually be observed from a completely different galaxy six billion light years away.

The true explosion followed. A superheated flood of thick sub-atomic soup chased the light into the void at thirty thousand kilometers a second.

An orbiting planet of space-trash floated innocently in the void only a few hours distant from the supernova, unaware of the tsunami of obliteration that shrieked and howled towards it.

====== [FLASH] ======

The moment both spider and human stepped under the shade of the tower's hatch, the world outside plunged into absolute, total darkness. Both creatures paused in confusion, blinking in the sudden loss of light. Light returned as a flash of limitless energy. Under the black shade of the huge metal plate above, Hemera Nyx and Araneo saw the world around them as pure luminescence.

Then darkness again.

Hemera blinked and tried to rub her sparking eyes behind her glass as Araneo tried to use his small arms against his own visor. The darkness began to lighten. The small lights of fellow prisoners, the safety lights of the central mining shaft gradually returned as a strangely gentle glowing returned in the sky outside.

"Wha-" Hemera tried to ask, then jumped in fright as a deafening electronic honking filled the air. Small lights flared and spun as robotic clicking echoed from the broadcast speakers.

`[!WARNING!]`
`[!EMERGENCY HATCH CLOSING!]`
`[!RETURN TO ASSIGNED STATIONS!]`

The screech of rusted pistons cut through Hemera's helmet, making her wince in pain as they ran back to the hole and jumped over the safety railing.

There was a grumbling crunch as the big plate settled into place as the prison camp #TTGL-OP-126 sealed its top shut.

======[UNDER COVER]======

The two small thrusters on Araneo's belt slowed his descent, but he still hit the elevator platform with a solid thud. Hemera landed a moment later in a puff of exhaust, her boots gently accepting the rusted grating as it squeaked under her weight.

The elevator had already shuddered to life as it began into the dark shaft of the mining spike tower. It was a straight line down, ringed with cold melted metals that glinted the elevator lights back at her. Bolted along the walls outside of the lift's supports were platforms, catwalks, supports, ladders, and railings haphazardly entwined the shaft. Hemera turned to the spider and waved her arms up at him.

"What *was* that?"

Araneo tapped the top of his helmet with a segmented leg in a nervous twitch.

[I HAVE A THEORY. *THOUGHTFUL* A HORRIBLE/TER-RIBLE/PANIC THEORY. *FEAR* WE MAY BE IN EXTREME DANGER. *THOUGHTFUL*]

Hemera crossed her arms. "OK. So what's the theory?"

Araneo paced on the elevator platform. A Short-Horned Grunter and a slouching Spiked Yellow-Suit stood on the other end, surprised by the sudden arrival.

"Did you guys *see* that?"

The Short-Horned shrugged its thick, stubby limbs.

[WE SAW SOME STRANGE LIGHT SHIFTS. WAS THERE AN UNEXPECTED ATMOSPHERIC STORM? *CONFUSION*]

"We don't know what that was," Hemera said. The Yellow-Suit nodded vigorously.

[WE THOUGHT SOMEONE TRIED TO ESCAPE. WE THOUGHT THE FLASH WAS THE ORBITAL BEAM. *CONCERN* WE ARE GLAD IT IS NOT SO. *RELIEF*]

Araneo continued his pacing, oblivious to the conversation. Hemera waved as she tried to get in front of him.

"Araneo. Hey! You big dumb spider! *Talk* to me!"

Araneo paused.

[GIVE ME A MOMENT TO THINK. *ANNOYANCE*]

Hemera crossed her arms and turned to watch the walls as the elevator continued to descend. In the gloom of industrial lights, other dirty, tired prisoners could be seen walking the catwalks and planks, dangling limbs off the sides, watching the elevator grind downwards with hopeless eyes, stalks, and other sensory organs.

Hemera's internal pressure had reached a critical level. Security

Lock One rose into view, along with a ring of rest-pods.

"OK. My bio-containers are super full and I *need* to use a rest-pod. Do you want to meet up somewhere later?"

The horrible sonic wailing of the steel platform grinding to a halt sapped Hemera's will to live as she tapped an impatient leg. Araneo continued to pace and tap, apparently still trying to think.

"Hey… if it's just a theory, is there any way to prove it? Like, can you get more information or something?" Hemera started doing a little bent-over dance, placing one leg in front of the other. Araneo paused, then scuttled back and stood over her, metal pincers clicking.

[THIS IS A GOOD IDEA, HEMERA NYX. I WILL ACCESS THE TOWER'S DATA SYSTEMS. *CONVICTION*]

"I'll meet up with you later!" Hemera had already turned and was walking quickly towards an open rest-pod door. Araneo's burbling chirps followed her as she picked up her pace.

[IF I AM RIGHT, WE MAY NEED TO ATTEMPT ESCAPE. *CONCERN*]

"OK, sounds good!" Hemera gave a thumbs-up as she ran into the dark, open doorway and slammed it shut behind her.

======[A MATTER OF TIME]======

The rest-pod was a dark, silent void.

Nothing happened.

"Uhh…" said Hemera, looking around slowly. After another moment there was a hard clicking sound, the grinding noise of two rusty metal objects sliding past each other, and the lights that still worked flared and flickered to life.

The rest-pod revealed itself to be like so many others: a single elongated room, mostly stained metal grates and flat steel walls to make cleaning easier. In one corner a small nozzle poked down from the ceiling, and at the far end of the room the biologics-console took up the entire wall, covered in switches, knobs, and small electronic displays.

Feeling her waste-overflow sloshing in her boots, she shuffled across the room to the back console. There was a loud *beep* as a foamy spray filled the room with dazzling bubbles - a few large bubbles filling the empty space, while smaller bubbles covered her completely, working its way down into every nook and cranny in a fractal pattern, annihilating every living thing it came across. It vanished as quickly as it arrived.

The biologics-console was a style she had no real context for, but despite her ignorance it looked old to her, as if several generations of technology had left this one long behind. She inserted her **PLOT** in the center of the console and twisted the handle to lock it in. Almost immediately there was a *whoosh* as the air inside the room matched her needs, and she could feel the worn-out gravity bulbs trying to reach her default settings, only to not quite get there.

======= [FAMILIARITY] =======

The rubber gasket around the front faceplate was stuck again. Disconnecting her gloves, Hemera made sure the latches were un-locked, then dug her fingers into the edges and pulled. A moment's struggle, and the faceplate swung wide with a puff. She let out a long, low sigh, then breathed in deeply. It was the first naked-flesh sensa-tion since the last time she was in the rest-pod, and she was unsure of when exactly that was. Letting her shoulders relax as the pressure around her neck released, she gently placed the helmet on the rest-pod's floor. Touching her face, she ran her fingers through her longer hair, pulling on the matted stray clumps, feeling the sweat evaporate on her skin.

The sounds around her seemed strange, like she still had her hel-met on but it was ten sizes too big. She breathed deeply again, enjoy-ing not being locked into a hosed air supply, even as the smells of the rest-pod seeped into her nose. Shaking her head, she focused back on the console, sniffing and rubbing her eyes as a monitor flickered.

```
======
[CRIMINAL: HEMERA NYX]
======
[SALVAGE WEIGHT CREDIT]
[-026354 KG]
======
```

She shifted over to the main section of the console and pressed down a button with her thumb. The rows of small black levers began rapidly clicking up and down, automatically adjusting to her food-needs. She released the button as the levers finished and started snapping the levers up and down. She finished her selection and pressed another button. There was a buzz as the nutrient display lit up.

```
======
[PENDING TRANSACTION: -004253 KG]
======
[!INSUFFICIENT CREDIT!]
======
[CURRENT CREDIT: -026354 KG]
======
[ADD PENDING TRANSACTION TO CREDIT?]
[YES|NO]
======
```

On the side of the display, Hemera found the worn-out button with the universal symbol for 'accept,' which, to her, looked *exactly* like a cute cartoon cat face. There was a *ding*, and the wall behind the console thrummed, clicked, and churned as it assembled the ingredients.

A stuttering shook the walls as the machine ground to a halt. The lights flickered.

"Oh no..." whispered Hemera as the room went dark, reaching for her helmet on the floor.

After another moment, the churning noise started back up as the lights grumbled back on.

"Haauuugghhh..." she said as her knees gave out. She collapsed backwards, landing hard on her life-support backpack, arms and legs splayed, looking at the dull metal ceiling as the lights shined in her eyes.

Propped up by the box on her back, she rolled her head around. Her left shoulder ached as she tried to block out the light from above.

The situation seemed familiar.

======[TOO YOUNG TO BE THIS OLD]======

Even the temperature of the water felt uncomfortable as it oscillated between lukecool and lukewarm, providing no pleasure to her naked wetness as she ran her tired hands over herself, trying to remove the oily, gunky buildup off her skin and out of her hair.

The angry red scar tissue on her chest stung. She grimaced, bringing a pleading hand up to cover the old wound as the slimy water washed over it. Like voices joining a chorus, every injury she'd had began flaring up. The bones in her hand that had knit back together slightly off. The tight ache in her left shoulder, always subtly in the background of her awareness.

The console beeped. Hemera's lost attention was yanked back to reality as the nutrient tubes filled. Her stomach took control of her higher functions as she got back on her unsteady feet, unsure of when exactly she had sat down on the shower grate, only to panic towards the waste disposal chute as a liquid rumbling hit her bowels so loudly it echoed in the small space.

======[PRISON X6]======

Feeling relief from her digestive-emergency, she chewed her food slurry as fast as her fatigue would allow, glad for a chance to use her jaw and teeth instead of sucking through her helmet's feeding tube again.

The decrepit timer over the wide door continued to count down. Rest-pod visits were limited to prevent prisoners from permanently living inside of them. It didn't make any sense to her when she first arrived, but now the safety and joy of not being directly threatened by Trash-Heap made living in a stinking rest-pod seem like a valid lifestyle choice.

Taking a slow, deep breath, she sleepily tried to enjoy the time outside of her spacesuit. Chewing on some firmer chunks more slowly, she let herself slink back down the wall until she was sitting on the grated floor, then kept going, curling up into a fetal position as recycled water continued to drizzle down on her.

The food was mostly tasteless, something Hemera was glad for given that its basic constituents were locally sourced. She swallowed the rest of the chunky mush and whispered softly to herself.

"So this is adventure."

She laughed softly at the memory of a lifetime ago - a curly-headed child howling freedom in the cramped cockpit of a tiny, stolen maintenance spacecraft.

Freedom.

She was a prisoner inside her spacesuit, inside a rest-pod, inside a prison camp on a deadly planet, inside a vindictive galactic government, and all inside the endless, deadly void.

She always returned, in those tired, unguarded moments: fire and smoke, dotted and sparkling with the bodies of her friends. A rifle bolt punching through a clear visor, eye stalks holding her to an impossible promise. Her eyes traced her helmet as it rested across from her. Beyond the miracle of her cracked visor not shattering from all the extreme pressure changes, she could see a new hairline along the royal stamp at the base of the neck. With the dents and the faded and chipped paint, it looked like it had been deep-roasted and tossed through several meat grinders.

Resting her head, her eyes closing under their own weight, she felt the exhaustion roll over her like a warm, heavy blanket. She nearly gave in. The thinnest layer of self-awareness separated her from her desperately needed rest, the clock ticking down, fading, forgotten, until...

The smallest of rustling sounds caught her ear. She blurredly peeked through one half-closed eyelid at a figure propped up on the other side of the pod. A blackened skeleton. Her stained spacesuit and cracked helmet piled up next to the dry bones, dusted in soot, the flesh long dissolved into inert carbon. Her bony hand rested on the grated floor, open palm an invitation as the smooth, dark skull looked back at her, smiling peacefully.

Hemera closed her eyes and took a deep breath, then forced herself to her knees. Using the wall for support, she shoved herself resentfully upright as she glanced back in the corner.

Dead Hemera was gone.

There was no relief. There was no sadness. It had been a long time since she had felt anything beyond a numb sort of acceptance to the destiny that spread before her - endless, eternal, and as cold as the void itself.

======[THE BINDING SHIELD]======

She grunted as she checked the clock again, then checked her upside-down boots. The small streams of drops were evidence that they had not completely dried yet. She grunted again as she pulled her fabric spacesuit off the ceiling anchor and gave it a final rubdown with her fingers before slipping it on.

The lining of her spacesuit was a fabric-like mesh except at the joints, where it was rougher, hardened padding. The mesh kept the bare minimum air circulating around her skin as it regulated temperature and moisture, but also rubbed most of the hair off her body, something she grumbled about as she harassed a painfully ingrown hair.

Leaning against one of the stained metal walls, Hemera finished shoving her feet into her still-wet kickers. They had a much thicker padded mesh inside, a necessity for absorbing some of the shock from her occasional rocket-propelled landings. Another moment passed as she stepped into the struts, motors, and plates that made up her external skeleton. The joint-connectors required a bit of push and wiggle to connect to her suit through the gunky buildup. Clicking the knee-buttons, her eight little rocket-boot tubes popped out wiggling, cleaning themselves by spraying the sterilized gunk out in dusty geysers, making her cough a little.

Next, her life-support system, connected to the console via flexible hoses. It only took a moment to disconnect the hoses and swing it over her shoulders. It was heavy, like it always was after a refuel. She felt her shoulders tensing up again as the automated connections clicked and snapped and the straps folded down, clicking together in front of her chest, awaiting her **PLOT** device.

She glanced at that mysterious alien technology sticking out of the connection port as she put on her right glove. A small light on the console was glowing, indicating that it had finished charging. The lights of the room dulled and the wheezing air circulation cut off with a *clank* as she extracted the flat, boxy unit. She studied it in the gloom, passing a tired hand over the smoothly patterned surface as her forearm display lit up.

<pre>
                  ======
      [POWER LANGUAGE ORGANIC TRANSPONDER]
                  ======
             [NAME: HEMERA NYX]
           [CIN: G-FN-RA-12-9799-5]
               [STATUS: ALIVE]
                  ======
</pre>

Her eyes lingered on her status.

The **PLOT** slid in her chestplate easily, and there was a satisfying click as she locked the handle. The wheezing, clicking, flowing sounds increased as her suit switched from embedded low-powered batteries to run directly off the **PLOT**. Locking rings on her boots snapped together while she mindlessly cycled through system checks.

Rubbing her head, her fingers scratching and pulling at her longer hair, she traced the bald spots where her helmet's padding endlessly rubbed, then scratched over her entire scalp one last time. Wiggling her toes at the slight breeze drying her boots from within, she connected the other glove.

The only thing left was the helmet. Hemera picked it up and gave it another look, poking at the thin lines of repair tape she'd melted on the cracks in the glass. She ran a gloved finger along the rubber gaskets before testing the hinges.

She didn't want to put it on.

She never wanted to put it on.

Her helmet offered nothing but choking claustrophobia, a life-saving trap she could never escape from. It was a funeral suit for a corpse that refused to die, her heart still beating out of pure stubborn habit. She spoke softly into the empty of her head-bucket.

"I want to go home."

Her voice answered with someone else's words.

"What's slowing you down, kid?"

She rubbed a small stabbing pain in her head as she repeated it. It surprised her, the line she'd heard somewhere... *before*. It was a fragment, a flashing shard from her shattered past.

"So what's... slowing you down... kid?"

Hemera shoved her helmet on. The helmet base connected to the metal ring at the top of her suit's neck, and she grimaced as the rubber neck piece strongly tightened around her throat. The helmet padding inflated, anchoring itself against those bald spots. Finally, the flat of her hand brought the front around and pressed, her other hand snapping the latches shut. There was another hard *click* as air rushed into the small space between her face and the visor, and she released her unconsciously held breath.

Her cloak was full of holes, the corrosive drips and air relentless eroding the edges. It wasn't worth trying to fix with repair tape, but Hemera couldn't seem to part with it. She threw it vindictively over herself as she checked her display, then tapped the small button on the front of her air exchange, expelling some air in front of her, trying to get the smell out.

```
        ==   ====
   [OPEN: YE S][SOAP: OFF]
        =  ======
   [GRAV: 0.   [PLOT: 999]
   [TEMP: 028  LIFE: 998]
   [ATMO: 1.2]  SRA: 972]
        ====  =
   [12048:08:01   05:18]
        =======
```

The clock clicked to zero. The room filled with rainbow bubbles thick in the places she had touched, then vanished as the room hissed. The disgusting metal door flew open with a loud bang. A large, three-armed alien in a hard, articulated black spacesuit rushed into the room, threw its own cloak against the far wall, and yelled at her to get the hell out.

====== [EXPANSION] ======

Eighty thousand years ago, half of a derelict space station had been unceremoniously dumped in a long-forgotten corner of the galaxy. By chance, the half-kilometer thick hull had missed the only other gravitational pull in the system. Leaving Trash-Heap behind, it rolled along in a spiraling orbital decay towards the inevitable absorption by the distant star, speeding and tumbling alone in the dark.

But now the darkness had vanished. An expanding orb of light and power grew as the station's hull glowed in red, then orange, then white. Consumed entirely, it only took a three nanoseconds for the thick, ancient structure to flare and evaporate in the tsunami of energy and particles that engulfed it. The sub-atomic structure of its constituent atoms were obliterated, wiping the lost structure from existence itself. The supernova continued to roar through the void, oblivious to the speck of dust that flared and vanished.

The small metal planet continued to orbit, shining ever-so-slightly brighter in the night.

======[THE SITUATION]======

Hemera yawned and stretched as she turned to walk, giving a half-hearted scratch at her armpit as she spotted three short creatures headed her way. She lit up, a wide smile on her face.

"Apple! Pinky! Patches!"

They smiled toothy animal-smiles through star-patterned helmets and waved small paws in the air, a greeting which Hemera returned happily. They almost didn't seem like aliens to Hemera - they were too damn *cute* compared to the more common apes, octopuses, and arthropods. Fluffy, furry faces with round, perky ears smiled back at her through their patterned glass visors, all wet noses and short glowing rainbow horns, their bright eyes strikingly large as they sparkled in the gloom.

"Where's Shadow?"

Apple, the leader of the group, had a stunning gray-and-white wave-pattern on her fur. She stood in front of the other two with stubby arms held high.

[HUG! *DEMAND*]

"*Aww...* I got hugs for *all* you guys." Hemera wrapped her tired arms around Apple, feeling the soft *smoosh* of thick, soft fur under the spacesuit. Next came Patches, who had white fur with splotches of orange and black. Pinky's fur was a deeply rich shade of pink. She gave each one an extra hug as they gleefully gathered around her, squeaking excitedly. Hemera felt water at the edges of her eyes at being near her friends. Patches did a little dance, wiggling her little stubby patched-up space-suited tail as she spun and hopped out of the embrace.

[HEMERA NYX IS THE BEST HUG/HUGGER IN THE GAL-AXY/UNIVERSE. *CELEBRATION*]

Hemera felt a big smile on her face despite herself, her cheeks turning red. "*Awww!* Sounds like you guys want another -"

Apples stepped in, waving a negative paw to stop the celebration as she squeaked.

[FRIEND/ARANEO BELIEVES OUR NEARBY STAR HAS EX-PLODED INTO A SUPERNOVA AND WILL SOON OBLITER-ATE THE PLANET. *URGENCY*]

Hemera stepped back. "What?... is *that* what..."

The three aliens grew more agitated.

[DID YOU OBSERVE SUCH A THING? *QUESTION*]

"We were outside, on the top of the tower. It went dark, then there was this insane *flash*, and then..." Cold sweat filled Hemera's spacesuit. The cute creatures conferred with each other, the affection-ate feelings gone. Hemera leaned over the railing, looking up at the elevator platform above them.

"Hey, where is he now? *Where is Araneo?*"

Patches huffed and pointed a little round finger down the elevator shaft. The view down the deep shaft looked like a hole into the abyss.

[THE BOTTOM. WITH SHADOW. *STATEMENT*]

Pinky nodded and squeaked.

[ARANEO AND SHADOW ARE GOING TO ACCESS THE PRISON'S COMMUNICATION WITH THE OBSERVER THROUGH A SUBROUTINE TO BYPASS SECURITY. THE ORBITAL STATION WILL HAVE A CLEAR VIEW OF THE SOLAR DISTURBANCE TO VERIFY. THEN SHADOW TOLD US TO FIND YOU AND TELL YOU ALL OF THIS. *EXPLANATION*]

The tower lit up with flashing lights and rattling alarms as the clicking robotic announcement echoed up and down the shaft.

[!WARNING!]
[!UNAUTHORIZED MAINFRAME ACCESS DETECTED!]
[!FULL SECURITY LOCK DOWN ENGAGED!]

The squealing, crunching sound of the tower's central security locks closing echoed up and down the tower as Apple turned to say something.

Hemera had already disappeared over the railing.

======[THE BOTTOM]======

The elevator shaft sped by quickly. The support struts and connections spun and flashed, the only visible evidence of existence as she fell.

The prison tower had started as an orbital projectile, and it still retained that basic shape. Over time, however, it had spread 'roots' into the surrounding ground. These tubes, pipes, vents, and sundry sucked the seeping organic matter out of the artificial soil and rock to funnel into the rest-pods. The prisoners, in search of viable salvage to pay off their debts, dug deeper into the planet, allowing more tubes and pipes to follow their exploration.

Still falling, she looked up to see another security hatch locking shut behind her. She had joked about the tower being alive, but it was in some sense - it monitored its own condition and sent work commands to consoles. Prisoners who did tower-maintenance would often find their salvage-weight debts lower. A few even said their food tasted better, that the tower rewarded obedience in ways and means invisible to those who fought against it.

It was getting even darker as she reached the fourth level. There was a reason so few came down here. The old impact left its mark on the crumpled hull and twisted beams that criss-crossed the drop into the pitch black cavern below.

Danger increased with depth, and it was extra dangerous to work in the large, curved cavern at the bottom of the old impact-hole, filled as it was with long unexplored tunnels and fissures that seeped, hissed, and buzzed.

The fourth and final security hatch coiled shut. Hemera turned and flared her boots, illuminating the final ruinous section. It only took a moment for her eyes to adjust to the light spilling out of the tunnel, just wide enough for a very big spider to scuffle through. She landed hard and ran down the excavated space. It didn't take long to open up into an ad-hock workroom or some sort of command center and tinkering space. It even had a large space-spider tapping at a flashing-red console.

"Araneo!"

Araneo jumped, hit his back on the low ceiling, then whirled around, legs wrapped around his shaking, space-suited body.

[HEMERA NYX! YOU SCARED THE FECES OUT OF ME. *SHOCK*]

Hemera's sudden chuckling ran into laughter. "Is it true? We're all going to die in a supernova? That's what we saw? *Hahaha!*" Araneo unwrapped himself and upright, unsure of what was happening, eyes peering through his glass faceplate, fangs tilted in concern. Hemera's hands trembled as she felt the laughing giving way to panic. She closed her eyes and concentrated on her breathing, turning up the oxygen knob, working to keep herself even as the existential hysteria flooded her body. Every cell in her body screamed to be set free, to escape this spacesuit, to rip off the prison that was keeping her body alive as it killed her, unable to breathe, gasping, screaming.

[IT IS TRUE. *STATEMENT*]

Shadow stepped out from behind a spider leg. His white horn glowed brightly, but his black fur was still darkness, the white fur patterns almost skull-like in the light. Araneo nodded in agreement and gestured to the console.

[I HAVE ORBITAL VERIFICATION. OUR CLOSEST STAR IS RAPIDLY EXPANDING. *CONCERN*]

Hemera's outpouring of emotions and panic slowly trickled to a simple light sobbing. She finally clicked the oxygen knob back down, feeling physically exhausted.

"How long do we have?"

Shadow shrugged as Araneo wobbled his head.

[I AM NOT AN ASTROPHYSICIST. *APOLOGY* IT SEEMS LIKE IT IS COMING QUITE QUICKLY. *GUESS*]

Hemera nodded at the ground, which seemed to be pulling her down more strongly now. "So I guess... that's it, then?"

Araneo moved forward, but Shadow stepped in front of him, stubby arms out.

[THERE IS A WAY OUT. *ASSURANCE*]

Araneo held himself behind Shadow, waving a leg at the fuzzy creature for emphasis, but Hemera couldn't hear past her buzzing head.

"Four security doors, the elevator platform, the top hatch - all sealed shut. That's a lot of thick layered steel. And then even if I got to the *Sparrow*, the Observer would take me down before I got off the platform. All assuming this happens before this supernova obliterates the entire planet." Hemera felt her jaw muscles getting hard. "So, *please*, tell me! How we get out of this?"

As an answer, Shadow waved her into a side-passage farther in the room. Hemera followed slowly as his stubby legs carried him into a small storage room carved from steel rock. A large object sat on a skeletal platform in the center of the room, and Hemera caught her breath at the sight.

======[A WAY OUT]======

It was a drill.

Taller than she was, the semi-transparent cone sparkled in the light of her helmet. The bottom was ringed in a pattern of wires and tubes, almost like little exhaust ports.

"What is this?" Hemera asked as she stooped to look underneath. Several mechanical rings separated the drill itself from the base, and Hemera saw the unmistakable hollow of a **PLOT** plug in the center.

[HAVE YOU EVER WONDERED HOW THIS TOWER IMPACT-ED A STEEL PLANET WITHOUT DESTROYING ITSELF? *QUESTION*]

Hemera jumped a little as Shadow appeared next to her. "... mmm, no?" There was something inside the drill, behind the ribbed crystal exterior, that she couldn't quite see. "So... what is this?"

[THIS IS AN IMPACT DRILL. *STATEMENT* IT USES A KINETIC/MOVEMENT ENERGY/EXCITEMENT FUNNEL/??? TO REINTEGRATE GRAVITATIONAL PUSH/PULL. *EXPLA-NATION*]

"It does what now?" She stood back to look at the little creature, then up at Araneo, who watched from the hallway. Apparently too large to fit through the door, he clicked and clacked the answer as Hemera took another look.

[THE HARDER THE DRILL IMPACT, THE HARDER THE

GRAVITY RECYCLERS PUSH IT FORWARD. *STATEMENT*]

"That sounds insanely dangerous." Hemera stepped back to take the full view of the machine. "So one of you is going to use this to, what, smash through all the security doors, all the way up and out of the tower?"

Shadow shook his head, then patted her backside.

[HEMERA NYX WILL. *RELIEF*]

======[THE DRILL]======

Hemera crossed her arms and tried to think as she stared intensely at the drill. She couldn't deny the tug of curiosity in her chest, but common sense had to have a say first.

Maybe Araneo was wrong? That flash could have been anything? No... no, she'd seen it herself. He'd even made sure to verify it. And it wasn't exactly something to lie about, right? No spaceship, no lightning storm, no orbital beam could ever be that bright. Nothing was that bright... except a nova.

Still, it was hard to imagine the danger as real. And besides, they were really deep underground. If radiation and such fried the surface, they'd be safe. They could stay...

She kicked a rock in frustration. Being trapped in a sealed prison tower on this awful planet was a death sentence, exploding sun or no. The supernova would obliterate the planet no matter what. And obliterate anything in orbit, too. In fact, it would wipe all radio waves, all records, all transmissions. Everything in a bubble light-years across, all about to be wiped from existence.

Her debt would be paid.

Shadow reached up and tapped on her elbow.

[I DO MEAN TO HURRY YOU, HEMERA NYX. WE HAVE YET TO FIND A WAY PAST THE ORBITAL BEAMS, AND

WE ARE RAPIDLY RUNNING OUT OF TIME. *URGING*]

The drill sat on its supports just high enough for her to slide under, but she balked as she took another step back.

"No way! Too big! Too heavy! You want me to, what, pick it up and carry it out into the shaft? Even this guy couldn't do that!" Hemera motioned to the space-suited tarantula that watched from the hallway, but Shadow was pulling on her waist now as he motioned for her to crawl.

[YOU LACK UNDERSTANDING. *FRUSTRATION* ONCE ACTIVATED, WE WILL STRIKE THE DRILL UNTIL IT THE GRAVITY RECYCLERS RENDER IT WEIGHTLESS. *URGING*]

She was under it now, looking up at the **PLOT** slot. The time for indecision had come and gone, but Hemera's hand shook as she reached for her chest. In the dark under the machine, the memory of four black eye stalks watched her, still and vacant. A punctured helmet hit a floor made of dead leaves. She grit her teeth as she extracted her **PLOT** and inserted it into the drill. There was a low thrumming sound as the machine came to life, followed by a loud ping as her forearm display lit up.

======

[NEW DEVICE FOUND]

======

[TRANSLATING]

... [...] ... [...] ... [...] ...

======

[GYROSCOPE-ISOLATED GRAVITY-ASSISTED DRILL]
[STATUS: CONNECTED]

======

The ember of hope ignited in Hemera's chest. The tiny wisps of smoke caught at the corners of her eyes. "I... I think it's working! ... now what?" Hemera watched as the rings rotated independently, keeping the **PLOT** handle still, then saw a pair of stubby legs trying to stand on their toes.

[I CANNOT REACH THE DRILL. *FRUSTRATION*]

Hemera slid out quickly, then gasped. The shape inside the semi-transparent drill was - *another* drill, one that glowed softly in rhythm with the thrumming. The crystal exterior rotated very slowly as the spirals, now lit from behind, spun gracefully around.

"What should we do?" Hemera looked for Shadow, who had padded over to the corner stacked with pipes. He dug around until he found a sturdy one and hefted it for Hemera.

[HIT IT. HARD. *INSTRUCTIONS*]

Hemera took the pipe and looked back at the beautiful, spinning, glowing drill.

"Do... I really have to-"

Shadow jumped at her, squeaking and chirping loudly.

[HEMERA NYX WE DO NOT HAVE TIME FOR THIS HIT THE ???/THING AS HARD AS YOU CAN RIGHT NOW! *FRUSTRATION*]

"*AAAAAHHH!!*" Hemera yelled as she swung the pipe down, hitting the drill directly on the point.

======[FIGHTING SPIRIT]======

WAM!

The pipe nearly wrenched out of her arms as the drill began to rotate. Stepping back, Hemera watched in awe as it glower brighter from within, the spirals picking up pace. It felt good to hit something that hard. Shivers ran up her arms and back. Air flowed into her lungs, clearing the dust and cobwebs. Strength returned to her muscles. Even her bones seem to solidify.

She hefted the pipe high and closed her eyes. She could see them.

Those awful split-banded eyes, a gloating pile of Bones that smirked as everything Hemera held holy exploded and died.

WAM!

An evil-eyed man, scarred and mean, half-hidden behind the bars of his golden helmet. The rabid snarl of a man choking the life out of a terrified young woman.

WAM!

An ornate helmet with a half-mask, under which the cruelest twist of lips, venom dripping from the wrinkled corners.

WAM!

Hemera was yelling as she saw the translation in her display.

`[STOP! LOOK! *AWE*]`

Her eyes cleared as she dropped the pipe. The drill spun rapidly as it glowed brightly and floated gently a few centimeters off the supports.

`======[SECURITY LOCK 4]======`

Hemera stood on a bent, dripping strut that spanned over the black pit below. Emergency lights spun and shone down from high above, looking like stars from the dark gloom below. Her boot slipped on a bit of slime as she tried to set herself directly under the security door high above.

It didn't work like she thought it would. It spun directly upright, no matter how hard she tried to tilt it. Worse, the drill was wider than she was, making it nearly impossible to see where exactly she was pointing. The spinning drill thrummed and glowed as Hemera lifted it gently with a hand that gripped the **PLOT** handle tightly.

"Now what?"

Shadow had climbed on Araneo's back, and the large spider had already begun climbing the railings and struts along the edge.

"You know that hatch on the top of the tower is at least two or three times thicker than these security doors, right?"

Shadow waved his little arms.

[USE YOUR BOOSTERS AND IMPACT THE HATCH AS HARD AS YOU CAN. *YELLING*]

Hemera tapped her boots gently as she started pushing the drill up. Images of her smashing into a steel door at full speed played in her mind. All bones broken... or worse, *splat*. Dead.

Araneo had climbed farther that she had gotten, and both aliens were vocalizing at her. She paid no attention as she tried to convince herself to speed up.

"This is... the dumbest thing... I've ever done," Hemera grumbled to herself as she pushed on her boots. The drill buzzed and spun, the vibrations traveling her arm a promise of mechanical power. The door filled the view around the drill. With a final yell, Hemera tried to gain more even more speed as she grit her teeth, ready to be pancaked.

Impact. The sound was indescribable. If steel could yip in surprise, it did so as the point of the drill punctured the thick metal door like a pin popping a balloon. The grinding, squealing sound of ripping metal followed, immediately increasing in intensity. The drill was halfway through, and to Hemera's surprise, she was fine. The unmistakable chill of artificial gravity flowed over her, prickling her skin under her spacesuit.

"*Ha! HA! HAHAHA!*" Hemera laughed and yelled as the feeling of safety overcame her. It was true - the velocity was being forced through the recyclers, which powered the drill while keeping her momentum set directly behind it. Yelling, she anchored her shoulder to the underside and shoved her rocket boots to full power, her howling lost in the sound of crystal drill ripping steel apart.

And then she was through.

======[SECURITY LOCK 3]======

Spinning and floating straight upwards, the drill was definitely moving on its own. All she had to do now was hold on.

The tunnel was mostly empty, with only a few red-suited creatures poking their heads out of their holes in awe of the glowing drill that moved like destiny upwards. Hemera reversed her grip, bringing her boots to the underside as she looked back at the door below. The hole looked like a steel flower's bloom. A small white-horned figure was suddenly tossed through and landed hard next to it, while a dozen red eyes looked up, waving thick legs.

It's not big enough! Hemera's wide eyes tracked Shadow as he pulled a welder and began slicing at the steel as a red beam tried cutting across from underneath. The drill was halfway to the next lock. Hemera looked up at the rapidly approaching door, then back to the two aliens working the steel below.

Shadow jumped back in alarm as Hemera slammed next to him, her **RAMA** already out, the beam slicing as she started running. She jumped and slammed down again, and again, and the section they had been cutting groaned once before snapping loose and falling into the darkness below. A dozen wild eyes looked up at her as Araneo dangled dangerously off one metal hook at the end of his leg. Hemera reached out for him as she yelled his name. A large leg reached up as his belt boosters flared to life. Hemera pulled on the leg as hard as she could as more legs followed, and Araneo scrambled up.

All three aliens enjoyed one moment of relief, and then looked up in unison.

[THE DRILL! *ALARM*]

Hemera had already blasted off after it, legs wobbly from lack of practice, grunting at the startlingly loud pinging in her helmet.

```
=======
[!POWER LOW!]
=======
```

Her suit's internal batteries had nearly drained just from the beam and boot blasts. Heart beating fast, her hot, dry breath filled the space of her helmet as fast as the machine on her back could work. A guttural roar escaped her mouth as her hand found her **PLOT** handle and flipped, bringing her boots to the bottom of the drill and pushing.

"It's less scary if I go down!" Hemera yelled to herself as she pushed her boots, ignoring the rapidly depleting internal batteries, imagining she was falling down instead of flying up - that the force of gravity would smash through anything in her way.

```
=======[SECURITY LOCK 2]=======
```

The spinning projectile popped through the thick metal like an explosive bullet. The impact thundered through the enclosed space as ripped and red-edged steel chunks sprayed up and out, embedding themselves in the walls.

Hemera descended upwards, ringed by glowing energy and shrieking air that spun around the drill so intensely it seemed as if the machine itself had grown in both size and power. The world was becoming a blur, but as she continued to press down, she could see the prisoners scrambling for cover. The walkways and ramps were thick with them, all apparently panicked by fire-tailed comet that shook the walls as it flared brightly towards the gateway above.

"GET TO THE SURFACE!" she yelled, her thunderous voice blending with the cries and explosions as she pressed her boots harder. Somewhere between her muscle fibers burning, her tendons straining, and her blood flowing, there was another feeling working its way into her body.

She didn't feel the impact. There was no reason to feel it. Problems, obstacles, enemies, thick steel security doors - nothing could stand in her way.

======[SECURITY LOCK 1]======

Hemera Nyx was invincible.

A hundred prisoners ducked the spray of nearly liquid metal that splashed upwards as a human, wreathed in electricity and fire, followed a brilliant spinning cone upwards with impressive speed.

How awful had she felt all this time? Was it truly her fault her friends had died? Their burned corpses floated in the void, strangled faces frozen in agony, the inevitable result of Hemera's so-called heroism.

======
[!POWER LOW!]
======

She tried to yell, to tell them to get to the surface, but she couldn't hear her own voice over the sound of the machine that was now rocketing upwards.

======[ELEVATOR PLATFORM]======

The elevator platform was nothing more than a streak Hemera did not see as she flew through it.

The five meter thick steel cap at the top of the tower lay just ahead. How many times had she looked up at it from below? How many days had she spent locked within the tower's confines, or scavenging in deep, disgusting mines?

Flipping once more, she pushed her boots to the maximum as once more she was flying upwards fist first. There was no drill anymore - it was just her, howling with all the pain, rage, and ecstasy in the universe, the power of her soul in her fist of justice.

And for the first time in a long time, Hemera Nyx was having fun.

====== [THE VAULT OF HEAVEN] ======

An explosive geyser sprayed from the top of prison camp #TTGL-OP-126. Ribbons of liquid metal sprayed like confetti as a blindingly bright drill shot like a rocket into the toxic sky.

The tight darkness of the tower vanished as Hemera's suit went dark. Pulled by the gleaming machine higher, higher, higher, her legs wiggled and waved in the thick air. In the growing silence, the impossible seemed more and more possible. The drill would lead the way. It could smash through the Observer, speed through the solar explosion. She could push the drill through anything that got in her way, all the way back home.

And then it was *too* quiet. She glanced down through her dark helmet to see Trash-Heap falling away, the prison tower rapidly reducing in size as other towers appeared, the flat horizon now definitely picking up a curve.

"AaaaaaAAAAHHH!" Hemera flung a dead boot up to anchor herself as she twisted her **PLOT**'s handle. It unlocked and popped out as she pushed.

The drill went dark. Hemera watched it take a curved line, now nothing more than a dead projectile aimed at the horizon, then gasped as a bright light flooded her helmet.

====== [INEVITABLE] ======

Hemera felt her momentum slowing to the moment of weightlessness at the apex of her journey. Inserting her **PLOT**, she let herself fall back to the planet, the inside of her helmet clicking back to life.

The sky was too bright. One hand covering her clear side, Hemera squinted through the darkened half of her visor, searching for a shape or something, anything that could tell her how much time she had.

It seemed as if all the sky itself was bright. She wondered if she'd be able to see any sort of shape in the sky. What was a super-nova supposed to look like, anyway?

And then she saw the curve.

The sky *was* the supernova. It took up half the sky, and then it was bigger.

And bigger.

The thick atmosphere felt heavy as her body continued to fall, the tower rushing back up at her, her open eye overtaken by the magnitude of the celestial display.

======[TIME TO GO]======

Hemera landed fast, caught by big rubbery spider legs as she slid on her boots along the ground.

"ARANEO! YOU'RE OK!"

[THIS IS THE MOST AMAZING THING I HAVE EVER SEEN. *AWE*]

Hemera became aware of being surrounded by other prisoners, all looking up, all awestruck. She glanced back up at the light. It was much bigger than it had been a moment ago.

"Hey! *HEY! WE NEED TO GO!*" There was no time to be polite. Hemera punched Araneo's leg as hard as she could as she ran under him. *"WAKE UP!"*

Hemera growled as she climbed the pile of spaceships, find the *Sparrow* easily as it rested at an angle on top of a much larger ship. Latched. Bubbled. Hemera grabbed her arm, stopping herself from shoving her **PLOT** into the console.

Then she looked up again. The concept of scale failed her. It was an orb... but if it was an orb, then she was an atom, something so small she should not have existed in the same universe of the power unfolding before her.

Her **PLOT** connected.

====== [THE SPARROW RETURNS] ======

The *Sparrow* lit up instantly, almost as if it had anticipated her return. The primary engine flared and boosted as she threw the thrust under her and shot away from the tower at an incredible speed.

"Now, *whAAAA!!*"

The *Sparrow* snapped and spun as a line of light sliced the space where she had just been, missing her by four centimeters. Pulling around in a spiral, Hemera bent the *Sparrow* halfway around, using the primary engine to shift her vertical axis as another beam missed her, this time by four meters. Panting hot, dry air in the dark of her helmet, Hemera braced for another volley. It had seemed so certain before. Two missed shots.

Is the Sparrow *too small to be accurately tracked?* Another beam punched down from the shining sky. Hemera tracked it off in the distance, landing with an explosion near another prison tower in the distance. Small dots floated and flared. Hemera sped upwards, watching the distant prisoners from the other towers, risking the orbital beam to escape.

Risking a look back, Hemera smiled in relief to see tiny ships rocketing away from her tower.

"They got out!" she whispered to herself as she pushed the accelerator as hard as she could, and the thin sounds of the smelly, toxic atmosphere began dissipating into a calm, still nothingness.

She shot through the last wisps of clouds like a metal asteroid into the silky, brilliant void.

====== [ORBITAL LASER HAIR REMOVAL] ======

Hemera was almost free. A few more moments and she'd be past the Observer. A moment after that, she could be anywhere else.

Another beam of light streaked by, missing wildly. It wasn't aiming for her anymore - it was aiming at the ships behind her, those still trying to get off the planet. Unless she did something quickly, Araneo and her friends could be blasted into oblivion.

But instead of worry, an calm smile grew on her face. She knew in her bones that her friends could make it. They'd be OK.

She was going to make sure of it.

"Where are you?"

Another beam shot at the planet, but this time, Hemera could see the origin point of the photonic arrow. The cannon was rushing up so quickly, Hemera almost missed as she shot the *Sparrow's* towing hooks out. The metal claws crunched into the orbital laser's hull as the cables reeled, sparkling and glowing as the spool brakes engaged. One snapped completely, sending the spaceship into a side-spin as she drifted around.

Hemera could see the large satellite, the sharp antennas and panels, the blinking of warning lights. The big metal bully firing yet another bolt at her friends. It was too big, its compensation-thrusters too powerful, for the *Sparrow* to pull.

The remaining cable groaned as it reeled the *Sparrow* hard against the hull. Hemera was acting on instinct now, following her most basic personality trait: cause as much destruction as possible and hope for the best. Placing a wary hand on the flat of her visor, Hemera decompressed the cockpit, sighing in relief as yet again the glass held.

The supernova was even more impressive from orbit. It was enthralling, encompassing her by volume and gravitas: this was the fire of the gods.

The Observer bumped into her as it adjusted the beam, rescuing Hemera from being awestruck. It only took a moment to scramble out of the cockpit and stomp down the underside of her craft, giving her cutting laser a hard tug. The bulky gun extracted from the cavity, cables unwinding gently as Hemera hefted it at her hip and pointed straight down.

The satellite was far too big to cut in half, so she tried to imagine the mechanical innards - targeting computers, reactors, beam concentrators and such - hidden deep under the steel paneling.

She remembered a red line ripping across a Collected Alliance hull. Shaking her head, she shifted her grip on the cutter, then shifted again. Looking down, it seemed as if she had never actually seen the tool before - if she had, the proper way to use it would have been obvious, like it was now. Flipping it upside down, she hefted it to her shoulder. The boxy end fit around the curve, the trigger more easily accessible by reaching across her chest. Now she could see down the barrel directly. With both arms pushing it solidly down, she leaned forward and clicked. Her cutter bore down into an angry red hole, out of which smoke and sparks erupted like a volcano.

"One... two... three... ... four! ..." Hemera whispered as she focused on pushing the hole wider, wider, wider.

The solar event felt so close she was surprised she had not yet evaporated. The Observer's thrusters wiggled, then steadied as it tracked another target, bright tracking lights locking, the glow from the cannon growing. Small luminous cracks were forming down the *Sparrow's* cutter's barrel.

"... nineteen ... twenty... twenty... aahhhhh!" Hemera relented as she released and trigger and gave the cable a hard tug. The mechanisms pulled the cutter back into its storage box as she leaped for the cockpit, slammed the hatch, and sped off as fast as she could.

She held her breath as the orbital laser adjusted its position, the lens glowing as it charged a shot. And then it exploded. Spinning as she made distance, Hemera shouted and whooped in victory at the cloud of fire and smoke. She took one last look at the ugly planet below, glowing like a slimy coin stuck in the corner of the galaxy's ratty old couch. The shadows and glowing outlines of spaceships sped around her, each one a celebration. Hemera smiled at the spaceship

"What would you guys do without me?"

The *Sparrow's* primary engine opened in full thrust as Hemera tried to catch up. A crackling line appeared and stretched. And then another. And then more, as each spaceship dug into a tunnel and escaped.

"Goodbye, my friends."

And then she was alone. Behind her, the distant ball of discarded steel and slime was engulfed with liquid fire, igniting like a match head tossed into a nuclear reactor as it rushed after her, only seconds away.

Hemera had never clicked the switches and buttons so quickly before. Her fist slammed the button, and the universe stretched to almost fiction as the small spaceship snapped and vanished.

======[ALL THE STARS IN HEAVEN]======

"Uhhhhhhggggggghhhhhnnnn...?"

Hemera groaned as she regretfully awoke, unsure when she had fallen asleep. Her body felt ripped up after being worked past the point of all reason. It hurt to move, each muscle crying out in protest as she forced herself to shift in her seat, rubbing her eye with one hand.

There was something uncomfortable poking her in the hip. She shifted again and grumbled, then shifted again before her dirty, gloved hand began searching. It extracted something from a pouch. She held it up in the cockpit's lights for a moment.

"BLEEEHHH..." Hemera bleated as her hand shoved the colorful rock deep into her mouth. Then she paused as a single, clear thought rung like a crystal bell in her rough awareness.

Maybe I shouldn't shove alien rocks in my mouth?

"Plefh," she said, spitting as she pulled it out.

Considering the saliva-coated colors once more, she leaned back, holding the rock up high in the dim lights of the cockpit, suddenly glad it didn't taste like anything.

"I didn't even wash it first."

Resting the rock gently on her forehead, Hemera suddenly realized that she would never see her friends again. They had all taken off so quickly, there was no time to coordinate. At this point, they'd be light years away, spreading out across the galaxy, having their own adventures. She wasn't sad as she thought she'd be. Imagining the big spider and little fuzz-balls making their way through the galaxy filled her with a longing sort of joy as she leaned back in the saddle seat, suddenly aware of her surroundings again.

The *Sparrow* was, as always, a crammed mess of wires, buttons, switches, knobs, levers, dotted with screens and displays that beeped and glowed, but the view seemed different to her now, like she was seeing it for the first time. It was more than just the cockpit of her spaceship - it was the sight of freedom. Outside of the glass, the endless alien galaxy sparkled in the light of uncountable stars, each their own unique shade, color... personality.

Freedom. Freedom in a somehow still-function spacesuit. Freedom in her beloved little spacecraft, too small and nimble to be shot down. Freedom from any records she had been in that prison. Freedom in the galaxy, to seek out her own adventures where she pleased.

Pulling off her helmet, Hemera gave it a critical look. Chipped, dented, blanched, the metal bucket had somehow survived several hells. She tilted it, shining the starlight through the sparkling jagged lines running through the center of the thick glass that branched out on the top and bottom like branches and roots.

How many times had she almost died? Was it luck? Was it a curse? Adding 'get a new helmet and spacesuit' to her mental task list, she pulled around in an arc, the world outside awash in the brilliance of deep space, the stars far brighter than they ever were before.

She was back in the *Sparrow*. Back in control. She embraced the saddle seat in a giant hug, an uncontrollable sob erupting from her.

"Oh my sweet baby, oh I missed you so much..."

There was no rush now. She let herself meld to the seat once more, then peeked an eye open. Meeting her own reflected gaze, she grinned and nodded. The flash in her eyes excited her. She sat back up and flexed her arm, trying to impress herself.

Hemera Nyx was back, and the galaxy was open for business.

The navigation computer chewed away at the tunneling calculations to an Outpost a respectable distance away from Collected Alliance space.

While she waited, Hemera cut and bent a flat part of the navigation console up, careful to not cut any wires, until it became the perfect mount for her colorful rock. As a bonus, it was right in front of one of the small bank of lighted buttons, making colorful, tasteless rock look like it was glowing from within. She nodded at the neat addition to her the cockpit.

"Neat."

She felt so light she had to check the gravity settings. Something within had broken loose or burned away. Something was different now. Her eyes flowed through the endless void as she pondered. Every mistake, every failure. The eyes of dead friends, bodies lost in fire. All the pain and grief still lived in her, clawing at the edges of her heart, threatening to drag her down to hell.

But she was still alive. As long as she had that going for her, she could help when help was needed. She could still stand up to injustice. She could still fight for her friends, to protect others from aggression.

Failure was no reason to stop being a hero. She'd fail more and more, in this galaxy of the future. It was inevitable.

A determined grin spread across her face. Shifting her view back out through the glass, outer space seemed packed to bursting with stars, planets, and Outposts. Endless parades of aliens in their space-suits, the imagination and engineering of spaceships and stations, the mysterious Objects, and much stranger things yet to be discovered.

Like that one specific place. Destroyed. The location wiped from memory: the thin surface of a very specific planet. It was the only place in the entire galaxy where she could live freely, without the aid of spacesuits and rest-pods. Where clean drinking water fell from a breathable atmosphere. Smells, sights, tastes... the sensations of a living planet, overgrown with delicious foods, thick with human communities, all potential friends and lovers. It sounded far too good to be true. And that, she realized, was exactly why she had to go. The spark of hope burned too deeply in her chest to ignore. She had to see it for herself.

The navigation gave a startling loud ping as it locked the tunnel to the distant Outpost. The first step to something greater.

"Now then," she said, a smile growing on her face as she clicked switches. "What was I saying?"

Breathing in the *Sparrow's* cockpit once more, she revisited her memory of a naive young woman proclaiming herself 'adventurer,' wholly ignorant of the pain, death, suffering, and loss awaiting her and those she would come to care for.

"No no no..." she said, shaking her sadly. "...that's not how to do it. This is how you do it!"

With the refined and dignified grace of generational royalty, Hemera Nyx pointed a naked finger forward at the endless starscape ahead of her, then ripped a loud fart as she whooped:

"ADVENTURES FUCK YEEEAAAHHH!!"

She slammed her fist on the button. The edge between reality and fiction blurred as the *Sparrow* crackled, stretched, and vanished into outer space.

End Notes

There is no easy path to being a self-published author. This "Breakthrough Edition" of my debut novel represents nearly five years of personal effort as well as the support from friends and family. It's not an exaggeration to say that I wouldn't have this novel, or any of my future novels, without their support.

My mom deserves a shout-out, given that she's been the primary reason we haven't fallen into homelessness and starvation. My son deserves an equally important mention - without him I would not have had the drive to achieve something like this.

My Patrons from Patreon deserve praise and attention. The following people have gone above and beyond in supporting me as I develop this authorship career. Please check out their websites:

Scott Roche
ScottRoche.com

Sam Washington
spwashi.com

Phyllis Khare
PhyllisKhare.com

If you want to be mentioned in my next novel, please consider supporting me on Patreon. All Patrons get a free eBook of my novels, plus exclusive content, access to the discord server, and more!

And a big thank you to Jon Wesley Huff for the excellent title logo design! Check out his work at: **JonWesleyHuff.com**

Ways to Support:

As a self-published indie author, I don't have the backing of a multi-billion-dollar international corporation. The rise of self-publication is nothing short of a revolution in the literary arts, and I'm proud to stand next to my fellow indies as we forge a new path for the art of the written word. That said, there are a lot of ways that you, the reader, can support the transformation of literature into a new age:

- Join my Patreon or Ko-Fi to support me directly:
ko-fi.com/rskrules - patreon.com/rskrules

- Write a review wherever you can. Every honest review helps not just with visibility, but also helps me develop my own writing. I can't know what I'm doing right or wrong without feedback!

- Visit my website: **HyperNostalgia.org** for my developmental editing and beta reading services!

- Visit **RSKrules.com** just for fun!

- Follow me on social media:
tiktok.com/@rskrules
instagram.com/rsk_author
threads.net/@rsk_author
twitter.com/RskAuthor
goodreads.com/rskrules
youtube.com/@rskrules

Questions? Comments?
I'm always happy to hear directly from readers! Email me at:
RSK.Author@gmail.com

...and stay tuned for **The Adventures of Hemera Nyx** in...

=======
[For my Dad, and his Destination: Universe!]
=======